The Tartan Conspiracy

Richard Grindal

G.K. Hall & Co.
Thorndike, Maine

Published in Large Print by arrangement with
St. Martin's Press, Inc.

G.K. Hall Large Print Book Series.

Printed on acid free paper in Great Britain.

The text of this Large Print edition is unabridged.
Other aspects of the book may vary from the original
edition.

Set in 16 Pt. Plantin.

Library of Congress Cataloging-in-Publication Data

Grindal, Richard.
The Tartan conspiracy / Richard Grindal.
    p. cm.
  ISBN 0-8161-5984-X (alk. paper : lg. print)
   1. Terrorists—Scotland—Highlands—Fiction.
2. Assassins—Scotland—Highlands—Fiction.
3. Highlands (Scotland)—Fiction.   4. Large type
books.   I. Title.
[PR6057.R55T37   1994b]   94–7339
823'.914—dc20   CIP

CHAPTER ONE

The tuck-box stood next to an old trunk in the centre of the attic. Heaped around them was all the lumber which three generations of a family might be expected to accumulate over the years: old furniture, chipped and scratched, which Ian's parents had been reluctant to discard, a child's tricycle, a dressmaking dummy, a rusty birdcage, a tarpaulin, and a stack of oil paintings of Scottish landscapes in heavy gilded frames. A sepia photograph, also framed, of Ian's great-grandfather, which he remembered had once hung in the dining-room, had also finally been banished to the anonymity of the attic.

The trunk was not locked, and after blowing away the dust which had settled on the lid he opened it. In the tray at the top, carefully covered with newspaper, lay his father's morning-dress suit. Ian could not help smiling for he remembered how, at least a dozen years ago, his father had grudgingly accepted that the suit no longer fitted him and had been obliged to hire one on the occasion of a visit to Edinburgh by the Queen. He supposed that his father had kept the suit in the trunk, hoping that after retiring from the sedentary life of a civil servant he might be able to lose enough weight to allow it to be reenlisted into service.

Beneath the tray in the body of the trunk he found relics of an earlier period, faded mementoes of his father's youth; the cerise and white striped summer blazer of his Cambridge college, the tasselled rugby cap of the 1st XV at Glenalmond, even the peaked cap of his preparatory school in Crieff. Interspersed among the clothes were reminders of his father's many but fleeting interests.

'Last year it was curling, this year it's rock climbing,' Ian could remember his mother complaining to him when he was a lad. 'Whatever your father's next fad is going to be, I wonder.'

Later the crazes had faded, but still put away in the trunk were the climbing boots, a Glengarry with the badges of a score of curling clubs pinned to it, a case of salmon flies, a camera with a battery of lenses, three stamp albums. Among them was a Gaelic dictionary from the time when his father had been to evening classes in an attempt to learn the language.

Ian had always thought it curious that his father, who by application and unswerving singlemindedness had risen to almost the highest position open to him in the Scottish Office, should have been so fickle with his hobbies. He decided that there was nothing in the trunk which could not be either thrown away or given to an Oxfam charity shop. When he turned his attention to the tuck-box, he saw that it was locked with what appeared to be a shiny new padlock. When she had asked him to sort out the clothes and other belongings which his father had left, his mother had not given him any keys, so he went to find her.

She was gardening. Fiona Blackie's gardening was graceful and ineffective, modelled on how she believed Edwardian ladies had gardened. Many of her attitudes were based on her voracious reading of the memoirs and novels of the Edwardian age. That day she was wearing the statutory broad-brimmed straw hat and gardening gloves and was cutting off the dead heads of roses, dropping them in a basket which she was carrying slung over one arm. Nothing she did when gardening ever helped or hindered old Jamie, who came in two days every week to keep the lawn and the flowerbeds in some sort of order.

When Ian asked her, she told him she knew nothing of a key to the padlock on the tuck-box. 'Your father must have hidden it somewhere. You know how secretive he had become.'

'Shall I force it open then?'

'Do. There'll be nothing of any

consequence in the box, but we ought to make sure before we throw it away.' Mrs Blackie smiled and Ian guessed that she was about to make a gentle joke. 'On the other hand, he may have made another will disinheriting us and left it there.'

Ian was relieved to hear her making jokes. His father had died suddenly of a heart-attack only ten days ago, and he had come home at once from Edinburgh to find her crushed and helpless, seemingly incapable of absorbing the shock. He had stayed until after the funeral and then returned to Edinburgh briefly, leaving her with her sister for company. Now he was back again, and, seeing her resilience and her composure, he began to wonder whether it had been necessary to take three weeks' leave to be with her. It might have been better to take her to live for a time with him in Edinburgh. Settling his father's estate could just as easily have been done there, for the family's solicitors had their offices in the New Town, not far from Charlotte Square.

Using a chisel which he found in a tool-box in the garage, he forced the padlock on the trunk. The hasp and the plate to which it was fixed came away easily, for the wood behind it must have been rotten with age. To his surprise the box was almost full. Lying right on top was yet another memento of his father's youth, a large mounted photograph of the 1st XV rugby team at Glenalmond. His father, standing at one end of the back row, seemed puny alongside most of the other players. He had not been a large man, but wiry and strong until his heart trouble and Ian knew he had played scrum-half at Glenalmond. The face of the captain of the team, who stood in the centre of the middle row, seemed faintly familiar to Ian. In the photograph he was smiling confidently and almost with an arrogance, as though the position was his by right and he knew it.

Thinking that the names of the team might have been written on the back of the mount, he turned the photograph over and found a letter which had been attached to it with a piece of sticky tape. It was scarcely a letter, no more than a handwritten note on faded blue paper and with the words 'Galashiels, July 17' in the top right-hand corner. The handwriting was full of flourish, though the letters were not very well formed.

Dear Andy,
Now that it is over I had to write and thank you for the support you gave me during my year as Captain of the Coll. It was a pretty good year, wasn't it, with the fifteen unbeaten, the eleven beating the M.C.C., your scholarship to Cambridge and two others to Oxford? The old man

5

has written me a most gushing letter of thanks to send me on my way!

I don't mind telling you now that last September I was shitting myself at the prospect of being Captain. Didn't think I would be able to cope. I was hardly a popular choice was I? But the lads rallied round and I know that was your doing. I should have realized that you as my closest and very special friend, would see me through.

Now we have to go our seperate ways, you to Cambridge, me to the army, but we mustn't lose touch. Don't ever let that happen, Andy. I shall miss you.

Yours aye
Sandy.

As he read the letter, Ian had the uncomfortable feeling that he was eavesdropping. The letter's boyish enthusiasm, immature handwriting, and poor spelling were a kind of reincarnation of a part of his father's life which Ian had never known and which, he now felt, was not meant to know. Even reading the diminutive of his father's name made him feel uncomfortable. He had never heard anyone, not even his mother, use it when his father was alive.

Beneath the rugby-team photograph was another, equal in size but in colour. In it a

6

crowd of young people were standing in a quadrangle, all wearing evening dress and all looking up at the camera, which must have been aimed down at them from an upper window or a balcony. Ian's father was not difficult to spot, for he was wearing his dress kilt with a Kenmore doublet, jabot, and fur sporran. Standing next to him was a dark-haired girl with a hawkish face whom Ian did not recognize. The photograph, he realized, must have been taken during a May Ball in Cambridge, at first light after the last waltz and before the energetic left to punt up to Grantchester for breakfast.

When he looked more closely he saw that another young man in a kilt was standing immediately behind his father. He was taller than his father and broader, an imposing figure among the other undergraduates. The faces in the photograph were too small for him to be sure, but he thought it might be the same young man as he had seen in the Glenalmond rugby group, the captain of the team. Next to the college photograph was an envelope full of old black and white snapshots taken on different occasions and in different places. In all of them his father featured with his same friend, on top of a rock face which they had evidently scaled, in waders by a river, in a sailing boat. Ian supposed that they must date back forty years or more when his father was in his

7

twenties and still a bachelor.

Suddenly, by intuition rather than recognition, he knew who the young man must be. Although his father had never mentioned the fact, he recalled his mother telling him that General Alexander Ballantine had been a friend of his father at Glenalmond. Once again Ian had the feeling that he was invading his father's privacy and he put the snapshots back in the envelope.

Beneath them lay a buff folder containing two sheaves of press cuttings, each sheaf neatly clipped together. One glance at them confirmed that his guess about the young man in the Cambridge photograph had been right. The clippings in the first sheaf were mostly from local newspapers in the Borders and must have been collected over many years. Through them one could follow the life of Sandy Ballantine from the time that he was a lad. The earliest one reported how he, the son of a shopkeeper in Galashiels, had won scholarships which would enable him to be educated at Glenalmond College. Another cutting, which carried a photo, told how he had passed out of Sandhurst, winning the Sword of Honour. There were accounts of rugby matches in which he had played, representing the Army and the South of Scotland. Only a posting overseas, one correspondent claimed, had prevented Lieutenant Ballantine winning an international cap. Not many years afterwards he was decorated for gallantry in Korea and the citation was printed in full. Another press photo, dating back some ten years, showed him in the uniform of a colonel outside a church in a wedding group taken after his marriage to the widow of a fellow Army officer.

The clippings in the other batch were all more recent and more sensational. One from the front page of the *Scotsman* carried a glaring headline: IRA MURDER SCOTS WAR HERO.

The report told how General Alexander Ballantine CBE, DSO had died while on holiday off the west coast of Scotland, when the boat in which he had been cruising had been destroyed by a bomb. The IRA had claimed responsibility for the assassination—a legitimate act of war was how they had described it—even though General Ballantine had never served in Northern Ireland.

Other clippings from the tabloids gave lurid accounts of the bombing, describing how local boatmen from the small town of Ardnadaig, speeding to the scene of the explosion, had found the General's mutilated body floating among the debris of the boat. There were interviews with people on shore who claimed to have seen suspicious strangers loitering the previous

9

day around the harbour where the boat had been moored. A woman who had served the General his breakfast in the inn where he had been staying said that he had seemed preoccupied, as though he may have been warned of the impending attack on his life. The vortex of sensation had sucked in everyone who wanted his name in the papers, his face on the television screens. Some reports mentioned briefly that a young boy, son of a fisherman, who had been in the boat with Ballantine had also been killed.

Also among the cuttings Ian found two obituaries, one from the *Scotsman*, which wrote in glowing terms of General Ballantine's life and achievements, the other, shorter and less euphoric, from *The Times*. The supercilious scribblers in London would see a Scots general as not deserving much space, Ian thought with a pang of resentment. Both obituaries reported that the General's wife had died three years previously and that he was survived only by his two stepdaughters, one of whom was Isobel Gillespie, the well-known writer of children's books.

Ian found himself wondering why his father should have collected and locked away these mementoes of Sandy Ballantine. He remembered being told that they had been at school together, but had not formed the impression that their friendship had been

10

particularly close. A few days after the General's death he had come home from Edinburgh for the weekend and it had been his mother who had seemed upset by the news. 'Wasn't it dreadful about poor Sandy Ballantine?' had been her comment. His father had said nothing.

When Andrew Blackie had retired from the Scottish Office and he and his wife had come to live in the family home at Invermuir he had seemed relaxed and contented. Now, he had said, he would have time to concentrate on all the pleasures he had neglected, golf, fishing, stalking, and of course his stamp collection. In retrospect, Ian realized, things had not appeared to have worked out that way. His father had gradually changed. Mrs Blackie thought he had become secretive. To Ian it was almost as though he had withdrawn into a private world, one of which he never spoke and in which neither his family nor his friends were welcome.

He delved further into the tuck-box, half afraid that he would find it was no more than a repository for sentimental reminders of what was beginning to appear as his father's obsessive attachment for his school friend. Instead he found an assortment of papers, books, and posters, none of which seemed to have any association with General Ballantine. An old copy of Hansard lay on

11

top and he saw that it carried a report dated some years previously of a debate in the House of Commons on Scottish devolution. He remembered the debate and the publicity it had been given. One of the speeches had been that of the current Prime Minister, Alisdair Buchanan, at that time a back-bencher. Himself a Scot, he had spoken with passion of Scotland's right for self-government. Now, as his critics from north of the border were always reminding him, that passion had become strangely muted.

Next to the Hansard was an Ordnance Survey map, number 52 in the Landranger series, covering the area north of Perth, and beneath the map four books: *A Grandfather's Tales* by Walter Scott, *Inglorious Failure* by Gordon Strachan, and two books on climbing, one listing the Munros of Scotland and the other describing some of the best rock climbs in the Highlands. The Scott history, though worn and old, was bound in leather and, thinking that it might have been one of the school prizes won by his father, Ian opened it. There was nothing on the fly-leaf to show that it had been a prize but on the inside of the cover a price had been written in pencil, suggesting that it had been bought at a second-hand book shop and, judged by the amount, fairly recently.

Inglorious Failure was a paperback with a

lurid cover, showing the flag of Scotland in flames against a shadowy background of Edinburgh Castle. Underneath the main title was a subtitle printed in what he supposed were meant to be letters of blood, *The Betrayal of Scotland*. Ian remembered the book appearing five or six years previously and that it was a hysterical attack on the ineffectiveness of the Scottish National Party as well as on the hybrid militant movements which nationalism had spawned—the Scottish National Liberation Army, Siol Nan Gaidheal, the 1320 Club, and a handful of others.

He opened the book and saw that it was heavily annotated and recognized his father's handwriting. Some passages of the book had been underlined, against others in the margin his father had written remarks of approval or scorn—'Quite right', 'Absolutely true', 'Inept!', 'Futile!', 'Unbelievable stupidity!' Comments of contempt heavily outweighed those of approval.

Even though it had aroused scarcely a flutter of interest when it had been published, Ian was not surprised that his father should have read the book with such interest. Andrew Blackie had always been a fervent believer in Scottish nationalism, even though his employment in government service and his loyalty to that service had restrained him from taking any part in politics. From time to time at home he would make a comment or, when he had been roused by some event, what was for him a short speech, which showed that he strongly believed that Scotland had a right to govern herself. What did surprise Ian was that his father should have kept the book locked up in the attic, rather than find a place for it in the bookshelves downstairs, where there were other publications, mostly academic and less emotive, on Scotland's aspirations for independence.

Beneath the map and the books, thrown into the box at random, it seemed, were pamphlets and leaflets. Among them Ian found a publicity brochure issued by the West Highland Scotch Whisky Company, which gave an account of the company's history, illustrated with colour photographs of its two malt whisky distilleries, Loch Maree and Glen Torridon. Next to it was the current *Annual Statistical Review*, published by the Scotch Whisky Association. Towards the back of the review was an alphabetical list of all the countries in the world to which Scotch whisky was exported, giving the volume and value of shipments made during the previous year. Ian noticed that his father had marked the entries for two or three countries on the first page of the list.

At the bottom of the box were a selection of posters produced by organizations supporting independence for Scotland, one of which, issued by Siol Nan Gaidheal some years previously, carried a drawing of a hooded man carrying a rifle and a dramatic quotation from the Declaration of Arbroath: '... so long as 100 of us remain alive we will never submit to ENGLISH RULE.' When Ian unfolded the poster he saw beneath it, perhaps hidden there, a Japanese microcassette pocket tape-recorder of the type used by businessmen when travelling, to dictate letters or file reports. There was a cassette in the recorder and another one in a tiny plastic box lay beside it.

The recorder seemed to be almost new and in good condition; too good to be left in the attic or thrown away with others of his father's belongings. Thinking that he might find a use for it himself, Ian saw that there was a cassette in the machine. He pressed the button marked play. The tape began to run but no sound came. Assuming that it must be a new tape or that it had been erased, he was about to switch the recorder off when suddenly he heard the sound of a voice from the tiny loudspeaker. The sound was slightly distorted as always with a pocket recorder, but he knew it was his father's voice.

'General Ballantine was not murdered by the IRA. I know that for a fact, but proving it will be difficult and may be dangerous. As I collect the evidence I will lodge it with my solicitors.'

CHAPTER TWO

Next day, as he was waiting in Kay's bar in Jamaica Street, Ian thought about the message on the pocket recorder. Although his father had known he had a heart disorder for some weeks, he had died quite suddenly from a coronary thrombosis. He must have recorded the message before the last, fatal attack, for he would not have been able to go up to the attic of the house afterwards. Why had he recorded it, Ian wondered. Was it because he had a premonition that he was going to die? And the message itself was strange. One should not ignore the possibility that Andrew Blackie had been suffering from some kind of paranoia. His mind may well have been affected by the murder of his friend Sandy Ballantine. Their friendship seemed to have been unusually close. Ian decided he would ask his mother tactfully about his father's state of mind in the days just before his death.

He had driven down from Invermuir to Edinburgh that morning principally to call on the family's solicitors, who needed him to sign some papers in connection with his father's estate. The appointment had been made for that afternoon and on an impulse Ian had telephoned an old friend, Bruce Niven, and arranged to meet him in Kay's bar at lunchtime. Bruce had been at school with Ian in Edinburgh and now he was a reporter on the *Scotsman*. Ian had seen his byline on the stories which the paper had carried after the death of General Ballantine and that was his main reason for wishing to talk to him.

When finally Bruce arrived at Kay's and they had settled down with a whisky apiece in the library bar at the back of the pub, almost the first thing he said was: 'I was upset to hear about your father, Ian. Should have written to your mother, but I have never got round to it.'

'Don't let that bother you.'

'Very sudden, wasn't it?'

'In a way, although we had known for some time that he had heart trouble.'

'I ran into him once in Edinburgh and he seemed well enough then.'

'When was that?' Ian asked quickly. 'Recently?'

'No, several weeks ago. He was coming out of the New Club with General Ballantine. And then not long afterwards I was sent up to cover the story when Ballantine was murdered. A strange coincidence, wasn't it?'

17

'Did you speak to my father?'

'Only briefly. Just to pass the time of day.'

By mentioning that he had seen Andrew Blackie with General Ballantine, Bruce had cut Ian off from a line of questioning which he had intended to follow and which had been his main reason for arranging their meeting that day. So they talked instead of Ballantine's death.

'Do you believe it really was the IRA who planted the bomb?' Ian asked.

'There's no proof that they did, but then who else could have killed him?'

'I suppose he might have had enemies.'

'No doubt he did, but private individuals don't usually use a bomb as a murder weapon. Bombs need organizing and resources and almost certainly accomplices.'

'Did you know General Ballantine?'

'When he came to live in Edinburgh after leaving the Army, he made himself known. He was always looking to get his name in the papers and his face on television.'

'Why do you think that was?'

Bruce shrugged his shoulders. 'He had always been given plenty of attention by the media. Perhaps he rather liked that and didn't want it to stop. We call people like that media junkies. But with the General I felt it was not just vanity but ambition. He was an arrogant man and felt that life had not given him the recognition and the rewards he deserved.'

'Are you saying he thought he should have been given a K? Is that it?'

'Why not? Many generals have been and his record was better than most.'

They broke off their conversation to order a bar lunch. Kay's was filling up with the rather odd assortment of regulars which one could always find there. Two elderly gentlemen, with the manner of men wealthy enough to have houses in Heriot Row but wearing scruffy cardigans and suede shoes, were exchanging crossword clues and answers across the room. Young accountants and solicitors, who would have been described as yuppies in the south, were talking of fast cars and Ayr races. A young woman in a red costume who was sitting on a bar stool was lecturing whoever cared to listen on the follies of the European Community's agricultural policy.

When they were eating their lunch, Bruce remarked, 'I understand that General Ballantine had been hoping for an invitation to join the Archers, but they were not keen to have him.'

He was referring to the Queen's Body Guard for Scotland, the Royal Company of Archers, an exclusive band of Scots who paraded in Lincoln Green with Robin Hood hats and longbows whenever the Queen came to Edinburgh. Many of the Archers were titled and a good proportion were former Army officers.

'I had always heard that Ballantine was popular,' Ian said.

'He was, with the troops and with ordinary folk. Larger than life in many ways. Good looking, an outstanding athlete and brave to the point of lunacy. "Suicide Sandy", they christened him in the army. But...' Bruce paused.

'But what?'

'It's the Hector Macdonald story once again. You should know. Didn't your forebears come from Dingwall?'

Ian did know about Sir Hector Macdonald, whose monument stood on a hill outside Dingwall. A hero of the battle of Omdurman, he had shot himself in a Paris hotel in 1903 rather than face the shame of a court-martial in Ceylon on charges of homosexuality. No evidence had ever been produced from Army or public records that the charges had been true and Sir Hector's only offence appeared to have been that he was a crofter's son from the Black Isle who had enlisted in the Gordon Highlanders as a private soldier. In Dingwall everyone believed that the charges against him were false, motivated by snobbery or jealousy.

'Ballantine didn't rise through the ranks and he was at school at Glenalmond,' Ian reminded Bruce. The fact that Sir Hector had been accused of homosexuality could only be a coincidence, but talking about it made him feel uncomfortable.

'No, but he was the son of a small shopkeeper.'

'Things like that don't matter today.'

'Not in the Army perhaps, but you know what Edinburgh folk are like.'

Ian restrained a smile, for although Bruce had been brought up in Edinburgh, his family were from Glasgow. The rivalry between Scotland's two principal cities was never very far below the surface.

'After his death, when I was doing a piece about Ballantine for the paper, I interviewed a number of prominent Edinburgh people who were supposed to be his friends. Without exception they spoke highly of him and said how upset they had been by his death, but never a one said he liked the man.'

'Did you interview his stepdaughter?'

'I did. And I had to go up to Wester Ross to see her. She has a place in Edinburgh, I believe, but spends most of her time in a cottage not far from Gairloch.'

'What did she have to say about Ballantine?'

'Very little. They were not very close. She's a strange lass, Isobel Gillespie, but a fine writer. Have you ever read any of her books? You should. My wee ones are mad about them.'

The conversation skipped into the subject of books and writers. Like every journalist Ian had ever met, Bruce had an unwritten novel hanging over his typewriter. As a lad Ian had read prodigiously, like many only children, working his way through Dickens, Walter Scott, and Henry James to Proust, Joyce, and Scott Fitzgerald, not forgetting Neil Gunn. Then, like Bruce, he had become too immersed in his work to find time for reading and now the only pleasure he had from literature was talking about it.

After finishing their lunch, they drank malt whisky with their coffee. Recalling the brochure he had found in his father's tuck-box, Ian asked for a glass of Loch Maree, but the pub did not have it among its generous selection of malt whiskies.

'The distillery no longer bottles Loch Maree as a single malt,' the barman told him. 'At one time we were able to buy it from Gordon and Macphail, the independent bottlers, but their stocks appear to have dried up.'

Ian did not mention the name of General Ballantine again over coffee, nor when they left Kay's and were walking up towards Queen Street. Bruce was a good journalist, with a penetrating intelligence, and he might already have been wondering about the reason for Ian's interest in the General. The question which Ian would have liked to ask him about Ballantine must remain unanswered until he found another way of satisfying his curiosity.

In Queen Street Bruce found a taxi to take him back to North Bridge and Ian walked round to the offices of Carmichael, Campbell, and Duffy, who had been solicitors to the Blackie family for three generations. Alan Duffy, the junior and the youngest partner, whom Ian was to see that day, was near enough a contemporary of his father, proof of the firm's reputation for an old-fashioned integrity as inviolable as Edinburgh Castle.

The formality of signing the papers was efficiently and amiably completed against a background of soothing reassurances that probate of Ian's father's will would be granted expeditiously and without any hindrance. Ian realized that his idea of speed would not be the same as that of Carmichael, Campbell, and Duffy, but money to cover living expenses meantime would not be a problem for his mother.

When the signing was done, Duffy said, 'I have a letter from your father for you, Ian.'

'A letter?'

'An envelope would be a more accurate description, for I have no idea what's inside it. It carries instructions that it was to be given to you in the event of your father's

23

death.'

'How long has it been in your keeping?'

'He must have brought it in when he was last in Edinburgh, only a short time before his death. I should have given it to you when I came up to see your mother on the day of the funeral, but by an oversight it was not included in the papers I brought.'

Duffy opened a drawer of his desk and took out a bulky brown envelope which he handed to Ian. On the envelope, in Andrew Blackie's handwriting, were written Ian's name and instructions on when the envelope was to be given to him. A piece of sticky tape had been fastened across the back flap, presumably to give extra security. Ian wondered whether this might be another evidence of his father's paranoia, a fear that even a firm of solicitors might steam open the envelope.

'Excuse me for a moment, Ian.' Duffy got up from his chair. 'There is something I have to do.'

He left the room and Ian smiled, recognizing a solicitor's discretion. He was being left to open the envelope if he so wished, without the embarrassment of a witness. Slitting it open, he saw inside an odd assortment of sheets and scraps of paper including what looked like a page torn from a coloured catalogue. Among them was a small, hard object, rectangular in outline, which he guessed at once must be another microcassette for a pocket tape-recorder. This was no time to go through the papers, so he waited for Alan Duffy to return.

'Was there anything in the packet that I should know about?' Duffy asked when he was at his desk again.

'I don't think so.'

'Not a later will disinheriting your mother and you?'

Duffy was smiling and Ian remembered that his mother had made the same joke when they were talking about the tuck-box in the attic. They could joke about the matter, because they were both confident that Andrew Blackie would not have been capable of such a bizarre mental aberration.

They chatted for a while, mainly about Ian's relations, some of who were living in Edinburgh. Duffy and his wife had been good friends of the Blackies and in spite of Edinburgh's size, social life there was restricted to small homogeneous groups of those who had been to the same schools or belonged to the same golf clubs.

Ian had no wish to prolong the meeting, for he planned to drive back to Invermuir that afternoon and arrive home in time for supper. He was saved from making excuses to leave when Duffy's secretary came into the room and told him that Inspector Reid had arrived.

'We have had to call in the police,' Duffy explained to Ian.

'Why was that?'

'Someone broke into the office last night. It was a clumsy attempt. Nothing was taken.'

*   *   *

When Ian arrived back home, his mother was waiting for him. 'I'm so glad you're back in good time, dear,' she said. 'Doctor MacBain is coming to supper.'

'You weren't expecting him, were you?'

'Not at all. He telephoned this morning and more or less invited himself.'

'Is the Black Widow coming?'

'You shouldn't call her that. Monica MacBain is one of the kindest women I know. No, she won't be coming. She has some committee meeting to attend.'

Nicholas MacBain was one of four general practitioners who had a group practice in Invermuir and he had attended Ian's father and mother from the time they had moved up from Edinburgh. He had previously had a fashionable and lucrative practice in London not far from Harley Street, but had returned to his native Wester Ross. As a Highlander and a local man, he had not taken long to integrate into the life of Invermuir, and he was popular. His wife was a Londoner from South Kensington and a thin, sour woman who, local people said, had devoured an earlier husband and was now making a meal of Nick MacBain.

'The reason Nick is coming,' Fiona Blackie said, 'is that he particularly wishes to talk to you; something to do with the golf club, I gather.'

'I hope he's not going to ask me to play golf.'

'He'll be here presently, so if you're going to, have a wash and change your shoes. Please hurry, dear.' Mrs Blackie looked reproachfully at Ian's shoes, dirtied on the drive home when he had to leave his car more than once to wipe the windscreen.

Ian did not welcome the news that Doctor MacBain was coming to supper. Even though the roads to the south were enormously improved, the drive to Edinburgh and back had been long, made wearisome by mist over Drumochter pass and a cloying drizzle after Inverness. He would have preferred not to have spent the evening in social trivialities. On top of that, in his haste to drive back home he had no more than glanced at the papers in the envelope his father had left for him. He had been looking forward to satisfying his curiosity by reading them at his leisure and also to playing the cassette on the pocket tape-recorder.

He went to his room and when he came

downstairs again Doctor MacBain had arrived and was taking a whisky with Mrs Blackie before supper. Ian joined them in a drink and presently Mrs Blackie left them for the kitchen to find out how Bella, a local woman who came in to help in the mornings and in the evenings when there were guests, was managing with the meal.

'I'm pleased to see your mother so well,' MacBain remarked.

'Aye. She seems to have got over the worst of the shock.'

'It must be a great comfort to have you here.'

'I think it is, but I will not be able to stay indefinitely.'

'What will she do? Not live here alone, surely?'

'We will have to decide that in due course. Meantime she can come and live with me in Edinburgh for a spell.'

'You'll have to leave the house empty then?'

'Why not? No one has ever broken into the place since my great-grandfather built it. Invermuir is not London. We've never even fitted a burglar alarm.'

Over supper MacBain raised the subject which had been his reason for coming that evening. He was the Captain of Invermuir Golf Club that year and the club's annual dinner was to be held the following evening.

The men's dinner was the chief social event of the year. A guest speaker was always invited, the cups and medals won during the year were presented, and the dress was dinner jackets or kilts. Ian had always thought that for a tiny Highland golf club, the dinner was an amusing *folie de grandeur*, but he would never be so tactless as to say so.

'The committee has asked me if I could persuade you to come to the men's dinner,' MacBain explained.

'But why?' Ian's father had made him a member of the golf club when he was just a lad, but he seldom played.

'We are going to pay a little tribute to your father and we feel it would be grand if you could be there.'

'That's a kindly gesture,' Mrs Blackie said. 'Andrew would have liked to hear that. You will go, Ian, will you not?'

'The club owes so much to your father. Two years back when we had to fire the secretary, it was he who came to our rescue.'

'He never mentioned that to me.'

'Aye, he straightened out the financial mess, arranged for an overdraft with the bank to see us through, got a girl in to do the typing. Do you know, he virtually ran the club himself for six weeks? We asked him if he would take on the job of secretary himself, but he refused.'

'Did he give you a reason for refusing?'

'He said he was too busy.' MacBain turned to Mrs Blackie. 'Strange thing for a retired man to say, was it not? One would have thought he would have liked something to keep himself occupied, not to mention a little extra income. Was he so busy?'

'He always seemed to have plenty to do,' Mrs Blackie replied. 'But what it was I have no idea. As I was telling you earlier, he had become so secretive these last months.'

'At what time do we dine tomorrow?' Ian asked. He had no wish to start a discussion on his father's behaviour in the months leading up to his death.

'Seven-thirty for eight-thirty. Just roll up. You'll not need a ticket, for you'll be the guest of the Committee.'

'Who is to be the principal guest?'

'Tristram Stewart. We were lucky to get him. He was captain of the R and A a year or two back, you know.'

After supper MacBain stayed on for a while chatting. Although she had been born in Edinburgh, Mrs Blackie had settled easily into the life of a small Highland town. When Ian's grandparents had been alive she and her husband would visit them frequently at weekends, and over the years she had made many friends in Invermuir, most of whom were known to MacBain. Ian knew them too, for as a boy he had spent much of his school holidays with his grandparents.

When MacBain had left, after assurances from Ian that he would be at the golf club dinner, Fiona Blackie said, 'I feel sorry for Nick. They say he had a wonderful practice in London. What a wrench it must have been to give it up and come to work here.'

'Why did he?'

'No one really knows. People have hinted that Monica made him leave London because he had become involved with a girl, a patient. I doubt that's true. More likely Monica wished to get away to forget that business with her children.'

Monica MacBain had been unable to have children, so she and Nick had adopted two boys. Both adoptions had turned out badly. The elder boy had become mentally unstable and had even attacked his mother with an axe. He had since emigrated to Australia. The other adopted son had been arrested in Bangkok for smuggling drugs and was serving a long prison sentence.

Ian too was inclined to feel sorry for MacBain. He was a pleasant enough man and, so everyone said, a first-class GP. Ian wondered whether he might have an opportunity at the golf club dinner of questioning him tactfully about his father's state of mind in the days before his death.

After his mother had gone to bed, he went to his own room, where he had left the envelope which Alan Duffy had given him.

Pulling out the papers from it, he spread them on the desk. Although the envelope had felt bulky, there was not as much in it as he had expected. The largest single item was a page torn from a brochure illustrated with colour photographs of houses and cottages providing holiday accommodation, giving their location, the names of the owners and the facilities they offered. Ian recognized it as a page from one of the brochures put out by the Scottish Tourist Board, which listed hotels, guest houses, and self-catering cottages available to holiday makers. The locations named on the page—Shieldaig, Torridon, and Poolewe—showed that the brochure was one covering Ross and Cromarty.

As he studied the page, Ian saw that a line in ink had been drawn against one of the entries. The photograph was one of a self-catering cottage situated some distance to the west of Loch Torridon. The house in the photograph was obviously a traditional crofter's two-roomed cottage and the description beneath boasted that it would 'sleep 3, with WC'. It added that 'own transport' was essential, suggesting that the cottage must be in a remote and lonely situation. The owner, a Mrs Smart, could be telephoned at her home in Inverness to arrange bookings.

The remaining items in the envelope were

equally unremarkable; a Scotrail timetable for trains on the Highland line, on the cover of which was written what looked like a telephone number, a rail ticket from Achnasheen to Dingwall, a receipted account for a night's stay in the Ferry Inn, Ardnadaig, proprietors Mr and Mrs John MacDougal, and an advertisement which looked as though it had been cut out of a local newspaper. The advertisement was for a store: Neil Mackinnon & Sons, The Quay, Ardnadaig; ships chandlers, boats for hire, fishing rods, bait and Calor gas supplied.

Ardnadaig, Ian remembered, was the little town where General Ballantine had been on holiday when he was killed. The railway timetable and ticket, the bill from the inn, and the newspaper advertisement must mean that his father had visited the town. The date on the railway ticket showed that the visit had been made exactly one week after Ballantine's death. Had it been a sentimental pilgrimage to the place where his boyhood friend had died? The question mark over their friendship still made Ian feel uncomfortable. He would have preferred to think that the visit had been part of the investigation which his father had mentioned in the message on the tape-recorder, but the notion was unconvincing.

He looked up at the wall opposite him. This had been his bedroom in the days when he came to visit his grandparents and which, spoiling him, they had furnished with all that would please a small boy. He would spend hours at the desk, reading and more often drawing, and they had framed some of the sketches he had done and hung them on the walls. He had always had a talent for drawing and had wanted to study art when he left school, but his father had persuaded him that accountancy would be a more sensible alternative. The sketch opposite him was one he had once made of Plockton, the little village that lay in a sheltered bay at the mouth of Loch Carron. Ardnadaig, he supposed, might be very like Plockton and, remembering the peace and beauty of the Western Highlands, he found it hard to associate it with the savagery of violent, premeditated murder.

He was tempted to put the envelope and its papers on one side and to forget them. The IRA had admitted responsibility for Ballantine's death. If that was untrue then it was the job of the police to find out who had killed him. In any case Ian was inclined to believe the IRA probably had killed him and it was only his father, obsessed with a wish to revenge his friend, who had conjured up a phantom conspiracy.

He was putting the papers back in their envelope, ready to bury them in a drawer, when he remembered the microcassette.

Taking it from its little plastic box he fitted it into the pocket recorder which was lying on the desk. It took him a while to find the message which had been recorded on it and he had first to rewind the tape. To his surprise the voice he heard was not his father's.

'Codeword firecracker. Andy, this is to let you know that our friends from across the water have asked for the meeting to be put back, but only for two days. Apparently the officers they're sending have had some difficulty in getting away. I have been assured that they are still enthusiastic about co-operating with us and they have promised they will still be able to meet both our deadlines, for delivery and for the diversion. The postponement makes no difference to me as everyone thinks that I am on holiday up here in Isobel's cottage and I had planned to stay on for a few days afterwards anyway, in order to divert any suspicion that it was something more. I have told none of the others about this change of plan, as we must stick to our rule about telephone silence. I suspect that my phone in Edinburgh is already being tapped. The cassette will be posted to you tomorrow and so will probably not reach you until after the meeting, but maybe you should get a message to the DMO. He has given me one proper bollocking already for not keeping him

35

informed. Biggest bullshitter in the Army, we always used to call him. You'll need to explain the reasons for the delay. Signing off now. Sandy.'

There was a pause of a few seconds, then the voice continued with a postscript to the message. 'There is one other thing; on my way here I had a word with the comptroller. I told him the rumour I had heard about funding, without letting on that it was you who suggested it to me. As it happened Ferret was there with him. They denied it of course. I said that I shall order an investigation when I get back and that if it's true I shall pull out immediately. If it is true, then the bloody idiots are putting our whole venture in danger. We had quite a barney about it, I can tell you.'

CHAPTER THREE

Fair Fa' your honest, sonsie face,
Great Chieftain o' the Puddin-race,
Aboon them a' ye tak your place,
Painch, tripe, or thairm,
Weel are ye wordy of a grace,
As lang's my arm.

As he recited the first verse of the Burns

ode, Douglas Hastie, the President of Invermuir Golf Club, had been holding the skean-dhu which he had drawn from his stocking poised above the haggis lying on a silver dish in front of him. Now he plunged it into the haggis, a little too theatrically, Ian thought, and made two cuts at right angles to each other. Then he took the three glasses of whisky which stood on the table next to the haggis, handed one to the piper and one to the chef, and raised the third one himself.

'Slainte Vhar!'

The three men downed their whiskies in a single swallow and the piper piped the chef out of the room, while the golfers clapped in time to his playing. The golf club dinner was being held in the Caledonian Hotel in Invermuir, for the clubhouse had no room large enough to accommodate the full number of members and guests who wished to attend. Ian was seated at the top table with the President, the Captain, the senior members of the club, and the more important of the guests who had been invited for the occasion. When the haggis had been served, Ronnie Wilkie Short, a former captain who was sitting on his right, pulled a face, took the glass of whisky which stood by his plate and poured the whisky over the haggis.

'A pity Mrs Macallister didn't make the haggis,' he remarked. 'This one isn't in the same league as hers.'

Ian knew that Mrs Macallister, like many women in small highland towns and villages, had made her reputation as a cook by preparing the haggis for the annual Burns Night supper, the golf club dinner, and any other occasion for celebration. Haggis could vary in flavour and texture from the indescribable to the superb and Mrs Macallister's were superb.

'Why didn't she?'

'You won't believe it! On a matter of principle; her daughter's principle. Did you know her daughter Jackie joined the golf club? Well, she's turned out to be a proper little women's libber and has been agitating to get more playing time for the ladies. She's been a real pain in the arse, I can tell you.'

'So Jackie persuaded her mother to refuse to cook the haggis?'

'Yes, because the Committee told her to get lost. Fortunately none of the other lady members are backing her. Pity about the haggis though. I resent having to pour a good whisky over an indifferent haggis. This is Loch Maree single malt, you know.'

'The other day a barman told me that Loch Maree is unobtainable.'

'The MD of the distillery provided it. He's a guest here tonight.'

When the meal was finished and decanters of whisky had been put on the tables to be drunk over coffee, the principal guest of the evening rose to speak. Although he had once held the coveted position of Captain of the Royal and Ancient Golf Club, the most important body in the game of golf, Tristram Stewart had been better known as a politician.

Eldest son in a wealthy family with estates in Sutherland, he had entered politics relatively late, winning a surprise victory for the Tories in Morayshire and holding the seat for some years, in spite of the popularity of the Scottish Nationalist Party in and around Speyside. After cutting his teeth on junior ministerial posts, he had become Minister of State in the Scottish Office. There he had shown such ability and diplomacy in dealing with a combative and discontented press that everyone assumed he would be made Secretary of State in due course, but only a couple of years back at a cabinet reshuffle he had been left in the cold. No one really knew why. People said it was because the Prime Minister, Alisdair Buchanan, was jealous, seeing Stewart as a rival for the leadership of the Tories.

Whatever the reason, Stewart had stepped back gracefully, and unlike other politicians who had been treated in the same way, he had never vented his spleen in spiteful attacks on the Prime Minister. Instead he had stood down from Parliament at the last election, refused the proffered peerage, and moved back to manage the family's estate and to golf. Though he had more than once played for Scotland as a young man, now he was satisfied with a regular weekly round at the tiny, unpretentious course of Golspie, near where he stayed. And his speech that evening, proposing the toast of Invermuir Golf Club was perfect for the occasion, neither patronizing nor fulsome, lightened with just enough light-hearted anecdotes of the top golfers he had known and giving the impression that the R and A knew about Invermuir Golf Club and respected it.

Dr MacBain spoke next, replying to Stewart's toast. His speech was irreproachable too, not as well constructed nor as smoothly delivered as Stewart's, but well suited to the occasion. He reviewed the events of the club's past year, mentioned its achievements in tournaments and competitions, thanked the Committee members for their help, and paid a tribute to the green-keeping staff and the professional. Finally he spoke of Andrew Blackie, whose untimely death, he said, had saddened everyone. He talked of his long membership, extending over more than fifty years, the many friendships he had made, the quiet, self-effacing way in which he had supported the club, and the tremendous amount of work he had done during the crisis of

40

management which all would remember. All the members present, he concluded, were delighted that Andrew's son was at the dinner that night, so that he would be aware of the great affection which his father had inspired and that all his friends were sharing his sadness.

Everyone in the room clapped. One member rose to do so and the others followed his example. Ian acknowledged their applause although privately he could not help feeling that the eulogy was a touch extravagant. His father had played golf from time to time since his retirement, but he had never been a committed golfer and had seldom taken part in the club's social life. Even so it was kind of Nick MacBain to say what he had and, as Ian's mother had remarked, his father would have liked to know that his friends were remembering him.

Two more speeches followed. A past captain proposed the health of the guests, who included representatives from golf clubs in Ross and Cromarty, and the other principal guest, a former Chief Constable of Tayside Police named Graeme Ross, replied on behalf of the guests.

When the applause for the final speaker had died down, Ronnie Wilkie Short turned to Ian. 'One has to say that Nick MacBain has handled things very well tonight. This is the best club dinner that I can recall.'

'The speeches were outstanding,' Ian replied. At most golf club dinners, the speeches were execrable, almost always too long and more often spiced liberally with lewd jokes that even a schoolboy would scorn.

'Nick was responsible for everything.'

'Did he choose the speakers?'

'Must have. They are both spending the night at his home.'

Presently the company began leaving the table, some making for home, others for the bar where, if tradition were followed, they would drink for as long as the hotel would allow them to. Before Ian had decided what he should do, he saw Dr MacBain beckoning to him. He went over and joined a small group around Tristram Stewart.

'Your father was a fine man,' Stewart said, after they had been introduced. 'He was the best writer of a brief of any civil servant I knew; lucid, economical, but brilliant.'

'He was a great admirer of yours,' Ian replied, and, thinking there could be no harm in being blunt, added, 'He always regretted that you did not become Secretary of State for Scotland.'

'So did I,' Stewart said, smiling, and everyone laughed. 'But maybe it was best that I didn't.'

'It's not too late,' someone remarked.

'It is for me. I have not the patience to endure Westminster again.'

Other members, drawn by Stewart's name and his personality, came to join them. Ian was introduced to Ross, the former Chief Constable for Tayside, a tall man with an imposing, almost intimidating presence, who, one felt, would have been more suited to dealing with the hard men of Glasgow than the gentle folk of Perth. They chatted about Perth, for Ian knew the city well, as one of his aunts had married a director of a Perth wine and spirit firm and they had a house beside the North Inch.

After a time the group became unmanageably large, and as it split up Ian found himself alone with Dr MacBain. Judging that there was enough noise of talking and laughter in the room to prevent any private conversation being overheard, he decided to ask MacBain about his father's state of mind at his death.

'I have been meaning to ask you, Nick; was my father being difficult in the days leading up to his death?'

'In what way?'

'Was he behaving oddly, erratically if you like?'

'Do you mean this secrecy your mother was talking about?'

'I was thinking more of what he might have said.'

'Why? Did he say anything strange to you, on the phone perhaps?'

'Not to me.'

MacBain seemed to hesitate, looking at Ian as though he had something to tell him but was uncertain whether he should. Then he said, almost reluctantly, 'I never mentioned this to your mother, as I had no wish to upset her, but on my last two visits your father's mind seemed to be rambling.'

'Rambling?'

'Yes, as though he might be suffering from some kind of delusions.'

*   *   *

As he approached Ardnadaig, driving down the steep, winding road from the hills, Ian recognized the sense of disappointment he felt, for he had experienced it before in Wester Ross. His first sight of the village as he rounded a bend on the moors some miles away had been enchanting, a tiny harbour surrounded by cottages whose white-washed walls were a dazzling contrast to the deep blue of the sea loch. Now as he drew near the charm faded, spoilt by the unsightly blemishes of neglect or carelessness; peeling paintwork on the façade of the inn, rusty cans and plastic sacks heaped on the quay, and in the window of a shop a garish poster advertising a soft-porn video. It was only a matter of time, Ian thought sadly, before the village had its Chinese carry-out.

In coming to Ardnadaig he had deliberately followed the same route as his father must have taken. When he had asked his mother over breakfast that morning, she had told him that his father had seldom been away from home during the previous few weeks and had never stayed away for more than one night. When his heart trouble had been first diagnosed, Dr MacBain had advised him to confine his driving to local journeys, for city traffic and motorways might cause too much stress. So he would drive to Dingwall or sometimes to Inverness, leave his car there, and travel by rail to Edinburgh where he would meet Sandy Ballantine. Since Sandy's death he had only once been away from home and had returned late the same day, tired and bad-tempered. He had not told his wife where he had been and she had not asked him.

After breakfast Ian had dialled the number he had seen written on the Scotrail timetable his father had left him and learnt that it was the number of a garage not far from Achnasheen. The garage had been his first point of call that morning and there the owner had told him he remembered renting a car at Achnasheen station not long ago to a man who had come off the train from

Dingwall. The man had wanted the car for just the one day, had paid the rental charge in cash, and gave his name as Andrews.

Driving to Dingwall first, taking a train to Achnasheen, and giving a false name at the garage, Ian realized, had all been part of his father's attempt to conceal what he was doing, to cover his tracks. He would have been irritated by the subterfuge and the whole seemingly juvenile plotting had he not known that his father had believed it was in some way connected with a violent murder.

From Achnasheen he had driven to Ardnadaig and now, as he arrived, he found a place to park his car by the harbour. Once there would have been fishing boats tied up at the quay, but fishing had declined along the west coast of Scotland now and the harbour only sheltered sailing boats; not many, for the season would soon be over. Few people were to be seen in the village either and none in the bar of the Ferry Inn, until a middle-aged woman, who Ian guessed must be Mrs MacDougal, came in and poured him a Scotch.

'You'll be on holiday?' she asked him.

Ian agreed. In a way that was the truth, for he was certainly not working, as his colleagues in Edinburgh would be aware. They chatted for a time about the weather, that year's holiday season, and the general decline in the hotel trade.

'There's just the one thing saved us this year,' Mrs MacDougal said, 'that business with the bomb and himself being killed.'

'Did that bring you much business?'

'For a whole week you'd not have recognized Ardnadaig. Reporters, photographers, TV people, they all rushed in. Every bed in the village and a good many outwith it were taken. You'll not believe the food they wanted and the drink! I'll not mind telling you, we kept the bar open past dawn. After just one day MacDougal had to telephone for more supplies.'

'Surely the press didn't stay here for a whole week?'

'Not at all; two days maybe and by then the casuals were pouring in.'

'Casuals?'

Sensation-seekers was what Mrs Mac-Dougal meant. Drawn by the press and broadcast publicity, hundreds of people had arrived in Ardnadaig, to stare, to talk, to savour the horror of violent death. Some had come in from other holiday resorts around the coast, some who were touring in Scotland had diverted fifty miles or more from their planned routes just to look in at Ardnadaig. They had hung around the harbour, talked to local people, taken photographs.

'Do you know,' Mrs MacDougal said, 'that one of them was even cheeky enough to go up to the room in which the General had spent the previous night.'

'What did he want?'

'He'd be looking for souvenirs, I expect. People do that, you ken.'

'Had General Ballantine left anything in the room?'

'Not at all. He'd only a small overnight bag and he took it with him.'

'When was this?'

'The same afternoon. Yon fellow was the first to arrive. Not long after the police.'

Ian had been afraid of what her answer might be, but he knew now that the inquisitive visitor could not have been his father. The railway ticket he had left in the envelope was dated a week after the bombing. As it was Mrs MacDougal had given him an opening to raise the subject of his father's visit.

'General Ballantine was a friend of our family.'

'Oh, aye?'

'You may have met my father. He came here too a while later because he didn't believe it was the IRA who planted the bomb.'

'What was his name?'

'Andrew.' Ian assumed that his father would have given the same name as he had at the garage and Andrew was near enough to Andrews.

'Ah, I mind who you mean now. A wee fellow who came in a battered green car. Asked me and MacDougal a heap of questions about your man: how long had he stayed with us; did he meet anyone here. Wanted to know about the boat too, so I says to MacDougal we'd best send him down to Mackinnon at the shop.'

'They had been friends since they were bairns.' Ian felt he must offer some explanation for his father's curiosity.

'Aye, I could see he was upset. There's no harm in that.'

'What kind of boat was it that the General was sailing?'

'You'd best ask Mackinnon that. He'll be in for his pint of heavy presently.'

'Can I get lunch here?'

'Aye. I'll be away to do the bar lunches any minute.'

Ian had finished his Scotch, so he bought another and took it to the doorway of the bar and looked out across the sea loch. Since he had arrived in Ardnadaig a fair-sized yacht had left the harbour and was heading for the mouth of the loch and the open sea beyond. Was it just off on a day's sail, he wondered, or was the boat setting out for Skye perhaps, or even the Outer Isles? At the sight of its white sails and its bow cutting the water, which he could make out even at a couple of miles, nostalgia tugged at him reminding him of sailing days in the past. He felt a sudden longing to be at sea too, at peace with the vast solitude of the ocean, escaping to an unknown landfall on some silent beach. Then he laughed at the thought. He had no need of escaping.

He returned to the bar and presently Mackinnon, the shop owner, arrived, just as Mrs MacDougal said he would, for a pint of heavy. To Ian's surprise he was wearing not the casual clothes of a country shopkeeper, but a dark blue suit, well worn but freshly pressed, and with it a gaudy tie reminiscent of the 1960s. Mrs MacDougal told him who Ian was and that he had been asking about the boat in which General Ballantine had been killed.

'You'll be a reporter then?'

'No, he's just on holiday,' Mrs MacDougal explained.

Mackinnon seemed disappointed. 'One of them reporters said he would be back to see me; told me he planned to write a book on the General.'

'A reporter friend of mine who is with the *Scotsman* was here. Bruce Niven. You may have met him.'

'Aye, no doubt. They all wished to interview me, and the photographs they took! In the shop, on the quay, in a boat making out as though I had just come back from searching for the body. Scottish

Television filmed me and it was on the news that very night. Did you happen to see it?'

'No, I believe I was travelling at the time.'

'A pity. They were very pleased with it.'

Ian suddenly realized that Mackinnon had enjoyed the way he had been thrust into a brief fame and was hoping even now that it was not all over. That was why he was wearing his suit. They talked a little longer about the bombing and the publicity it had been given. The boat, Mackinnon told him, had been a complete write-off, its engine at the bottom of the sea, the hull shattered into fragments.

'What kind of boat was it?'

'A motor cruiser. A fine vessel. The insurers are still haggling with the owners over its value.'

'You didn't own it then?'

'What would I need a boat like that for? No, it belonged to some folk from Sutherland, and as they could'na sail it so often I kept it here and would let it out for them, on commission, you understand.'

'Did the General rent it for just the one day?'

'No. Two days and he said he might need it for three. He wanted to be free to put in for the night at one of the islands, if he felt inclined to do so.'

Ian knew that he must ask one more question, a question he would have preferred

51

not to ask, as he did not know what the answer might be, but one of the reasons he had come to Ardnadaig was to learn the truth. 'I read that he had a young boy with him. Was he a local lad?'

'Aye. You see the previous evening, as I said on the telly, the General took the boat out for a wee while, just to get the feel of it, you ken. When he came in, he told me he would like to have someone with him who had sailed in the boat before. She was a powerful boat that needed handling. So he took wee Angus with him.'

'Who was the boy?'

'The grandson of Dougal who used to be on the ferry before that finished. He stays on a croft a mile or two away now. There's three or four lads always hanging round the harbour who'd have gone with him gladly but the General asked for Angus specially.'

'Have you any idea why?'

Mackinnon shrugged. 'Maybe he took pity on the wee fellow. Angus has been stone deaf since birth, you see.'

CHAPTER FOUR

Isobel Gillespie had a cottage overlooking the sea to the west of Shieldaig. By the time he found it, Ian was losing patience and had

52

to fight a temptation to turn the car round and head for home. In Ardnadaig on a sudden impulse he had telephoned Bruce Niven in Edinburgh and had been told that Isobel Gillespie's cottage was near Shieldaig. Forgetting that there were two places of that name in Wester Ross, he had driven to the nearer one, found he was wrong and had to return from where he had come. The drive to the right Shieldaig had been long and tiresome; first back to Kinlochewe along a single-track road that was both winding and undulating, then on the main road to the north-west almost as far as Gairloch and finally on what was little more than a path which led to a handful of crofts along the coast. Even on the main road there had been stretches which were single track and in many places long-overdue road works. The thought that no Parliament in London had ever shown more than a token interest in Scotland's needs only fed his exasperation.

Another reason for Ian's impatience was his growing doubt about the sense of the whole expedition he had undertaken. His father's inquiries into General Ballantine's death and the General's tape-recorded message were beginning to appear unreal, a fantasy into which he should not be allowing himself to be drawn. Knowing that Ballantine had been staying with his stepdaughter before his death, he had persuaded himself that Isobel Gillespie might be able to prove that it was not just a fantasy. But his real reason for wishing to see her, he realized, was a slender hope that she might be able to satisfy another persistent doubt and it was this that finally made him stop the car.

She answered his knock almost immediately and he guessed that she must have noticed the car arriving. He recognized her, for she had been one of the two girls in the wedding photograph of her mother and General Ballantine. The look she gave him was one of a patient resignation, as though she must endure this interruption to her afternoon as best she could.

'Hullo,' he said, 'I'm Ian Blackie.'

Her hesitation was only momentary. 'Of course! Andrew's son.'

'Am I disturbing you?'

She did not reply to the question, but opened the door wider. 'Come on in.'

The front door of the cottage opened directly into a room which, it seemed, was furnished to serve a number of purposes, but which was primarily a writer's room. A word processor stood on a table to one side and a portable electronic typewriter had been placed against one wall. The bookshelves had overflowed and there were small stacks of books everywhere, on the sofa, on another, larger, table, and on the floor.

54

Isobel cleared a portion of the sofa for Ian and sat down opposite him on a straight-backed chair which, he guessed, she usually used when she was writing. She made no apology for the disorder and may not have even been aware of it. Looking at her, he thought she had changed surprisingly little since the time of the wedding photograph. Her face was still that of a girl, but there was a maturity and a self-assurance in her manner.

'How is your father?' she asked.

'You will not have heard, but he died only a short while ago.'

'He's dead!' She seemed incredulous rather than shocked.

'It was not entirely unexpected. He had a heart complaint.'

'How sad! He was such a kind man, so gentle.'

The word was not one Ian would ever have associated with his father and he wondered why she had used it. Did it mean that she thought his father effeminate, and if so why? It was not a question he felt he could ask, so he asked another.

'Did he come here to see you recently?'

'No. Why should he have?'

'Your stepfather's death was worrying him.'

'Sandy's death. In what way?'

'Apparently he did not believe that it was

the IRA who had placed that bomb. So he had begun making enquiries of his own. I know he had been to Ardnadaig and spoken to people there.'

'You know that Sandy had been staying here with me before he went to Ardnadaig?'

'I had heard that, yes.'

'Does this mean that you are making enquiries into Sandy's death as well?'

'I suppose you might say I am, but not with any great enthusiasm.'

'Tell me about it.'

Slightly to his surprise, Ian found himself telling of the recorded message he had found in the tuck-box and of the envelope and its contents which his father had left for him with their solicitors. He had told no one else, mainly because he thought it might make his father appear as an eccentric, but he sensed in Isobel a kind of sympathy which invited confidences. He did not mention the codewords or the talk of telephone tapping and the faintly absurd secrecy with which his father and Sandy Ballantine had enveloped the escapade they were sharing.

When he had finished telling her, he added, 'I have been wondering about one thing.'

'What's that?'

'Your stepfather, I mean Sandy, had been here for a few days before he went to Ardnadaig for this meeting, had he not?'

Isobel nodded, so he continued, 'Then how did he learn that the meeting was to be postponed?'

'He had a phone call the evening before he was due to leave.'

'Do you know from whom?'

'Yes, I answered the phone. The man who asked to speak to Sandy said his name was Deeney, Sean Deeney.'

'Was he Irish?'

'Yes, but from Northern Ireland.'

'How do you know?'

'His accent was pure Belfast. I'm pretty hot on accents. It comes from spending a lot of time listening to other people's conversations. That's a writer's habit.'

'Did Sandy seem upset?'

'Not at all. I left the room, for I sensed he would wish to be alone. They spoke for a long time so I suppose whoever it was gave him a good reason for postponing the meeting. Sandy was quite relaxed; said he might wish to stay on with me for a day or two longer after the meeting, that's all.'

'If it was the IRA he was going to meet, they would hardly have killed him.'

'Unless it was a rival group.'

While they were talking Ian noticed that the clothes she was wearing seemed too old for her, as though they might have been borrowed or inherited from an older woman. Women writers he had seen interviewed on television had often been wearing unconventional clothes, frequently long, loose, shapeless dresses in unusual colours. This might mean that they were indifferent to their appearance, or it might be an affectation, a banner to proclaim their broadmindedness.

'Would you like a cup of tea or anything?' she asked him suddenly. 'I'm a crappy hostess.'

'No thanks. I've never really acquired the tea habit.'

'What about a drink then? Sandy brought a bottle of malt whisky from our local distillery with him. I'll never finish it on my own.'

Ian settled for a whisky and she left the room, returning with two cut-glass tumblers, a jug of water, and a bottle of whisky, on a silver tray. Here and there among the disorder were silver and glass, bowls, vases, ornaments which looked as if they would be better kept in a bank vault.

Isobel must have guessed what Ian was thinking, for she said, 'Edinburgh crystal and Sèvres porcelain in a crofter's cottage! It makes no sense, does it? But this is my only home.'

'I heard you had a pad in Edinburgh.'

'Some pad! A bed-sit in a married friend's Victorian house!'

'Have you never bought a place in the

south?'

'I've never had the cash. Writers don't earn half as much as people believe. And our family was never rich. Sandy offered to help, but why should he?'

Affluence and poverty were relative terms, Ian reflected. Isobel would never have known the squalor of a Glasgow tenement and even her cottage had modern plumbing as far as he could see. Even so he was beginning to detect in her an independence which he admired.

'Sadly I've just lost my pad in Edinburgh,' she remarked as she poured the whisky.

'Why is that?'

She explained that her friend whose home was in Morningside had just had a second baby. The room which Isobel was renting from her was needed now as a nursery.

'So I'll need to spend more time here, for a while at least.'

'Will you mind that?'

'No way! I love it here.' She looked out of the window. 'Come, I'll show you why. Bring your whisky with you.'

They went outside. The cottage was separated from the sea by the rough road that ran along the coast and a strip of marram, the sandy grass typical of the west highlands and islands of Scotland. From where they were standing one had a splendid view to the south of the Torridon mountains,

Beinn Eighe, Liathach, and the jewel mountain Beinn Alligin. But it was to the west, across the Minch, that Ian saw the sight which never failed to amaze him with its beauty, the sun beginning to set over Skye and the Western Isles. He and Isobel stood looking at the sunset without speaking.

'God, it's beautiful!' Ian said. The words were banal, but he felt he had to say something to break the spell of a shared emotion which was beginning to hold them. He added, more prosaically, 'You're lucky though to have a sunset like this so late in the autumn.'

Winter had been late in coming that year and even now the peaks of the mountains around them had no more than a dusting of snow. 'Winter's never really severe here,' Isobel told him. 'We have the Gulf Stream, remember.'

'I can understand why you should love living in Wester Ross, but aren't you rather vulnerable here?'

'People in this part of the world are not thieves and it's not likely that any stranger would trek all this way for my few trinkets.'

'I was not thinking of your valuables but of you; a woman living on your own.'

'One or two of the randy men used to chat me up in the inn down the road when I first came to live here. They may have had the idea of dropping in uninvited at night, but not any more.'

'Why is that?'

'They have probably written me off as a lesbian. I've encouraged them to believe that. One or two girlfriends have come to stay with me, but never a man, until Sandy invited himself, that is.'

The thought that she might in truth have lesbian inclinations paused for a moment as it passed through Ian's mind and he felt a pang of regret. Then he laughed at himself, but she had given him an opening to ask the question that had really brought him there. She was a girl who would expect directness, so there was no point in finessing.

'Might General Ballantine have been homosexual?' he asked her bluntly.

'A poof? Isn't that what you men call them?'

'I never have.'

She looked at him searchingly. 'Does this mean that you believe your father was?'

'It never even struck me that he might be, but recently I have begun to wonder,' Ian replied. 'He and Sandy seem to have had an unusually close friendship.'

He told her about the photograph, the letter and other mementoes of their friendship which he had found in his father's tuck-box. As he described them, he found himself thinking that as evidence of a homosexual relationship they must appear

61

slender indeed, but Isobel did not immediately dismiss them as absurd.

'And Sandy did remain a bachelor until well into middle age.'

'Yes, I know it's unfair to assume a man is a queer simply because he remains unmarried, but people do.'

'Sandy treated women with enormous charm, bought them flowers all the time, flattered them, though not to the point of fulsomeness, but I had the impression that he found it hard to love them, to become intimate. Even he and my mother were never really close. I always felt he married her chiefly through gallantry.'

'That sounds rather quixotic.'

'She had been left alone with two adolescent girls and a beggarly Army widow's pension.'

'So you think he was homosexual?'

'I didn't say that. Of one thing I am certain. Sandy would never have been a practising homosexual. He may have had homosexual inclinations. He may have been—how do the French put it?—a *pederaste manqué*, but he would not even have been aware of it.'

Ian knew what she meant. He had known men, more than one, who were plainly homosexual by instinct but had suppressed the urge, and who would have been horrified if anyone had accused them of sodomy.

Usually they lived with their parents or alone, seldom sought the company of women except on overtly social occasions, looked admiringly at other men, and sometimes would touch them affectionately but hesitantly.

'Would it bother you,' Isobel asked him, 'if you found out that your father had been queer?'

Ian thought for a while before replying, not because he had never thought about the idea before, but because he wished to answer honestly. 'If I learnt that he had been a practising homosexual, that he had deceived my mother, that would annoy me, no, not even that, I would just feel very embarrassed.'

As he was speaking, Ian thought how incongruous it was that they should be discussing homosexuality in the sunset, while looking at a matchless spectacle of natural beauty. Isobel may have felt the same, for she turned abruptly and they went back into the cottage. He realized that he would have to be satisfied with what she had given him, only her opinion and so inconclusive, but he had no reason to have expected more.

'You come from the borders, do you not?' he thought it best now to change the subject.

'Selkirk, if you call that the borders.'

'What brought you to Wester Ross?'

'I first came here with a boyfriend to spend

a holiday in a shieling.'

Ian knew that young people sometimes came to holiday in what had once been shepherds' huts on a highland pasture. For those who loved nature and had no objection to a life of bare simplicity, shielings offered an inexpensive holiday.

'And you liked it?'

'I fell in love with Wester Ross, but as an experiment in sex it was a disaster.'

'Tell me about it.' He used the same words as Isobel had when they were talking of his father, but sensed at once that he should not have done, that he was taking a liberty.

'One day I might.'

As he was finishing his dram they chatted for a while about the Highlands and about Edinburgh. As far as they could tell, they had no friends in common, but that was no surprise, for she had lived in Edinburgh only briefly. Then he realized that he should be leaving for home. Even though his mother seemed to be reconciled now to his father's death, he felt uneasy about leaving her alone for too long.

'What will you do, then?' she asked him as he began to leave. 'About Sandy's death, I mean.'

'I'm not certain. There is so little to support my father's suspicions. The sensible thing would be to inform the police, but I have nothing of any consequence to tell them. I suppose Sandy didn't leave anything behind here which would explain what he and my father were up to? No papers? No tape-recorder?'

'You're not the first person to ask me that.'

'You mean the police?'

'No, the police didn't, but a man called here in the evening after the bombing. He told me he was Sandy's driver and that he was supposed to pick up some papers that Sandy wanted him to take to his bank in Edinburgh.'

'And what did you say?'

Isobel's answer was prompt, almost curt. 'If Sandy had left anything here, I would not have told that man.'

'Why not?'

'He was lying. When Sandy arrived here, he complained about the journey from Edinburgh and the awful roads. He said he had been spoilt by Army life and how he wished he still had a driver to take him around.'

They were standing at the door of the cottage now. He asked her, 'Who do you suppose the man was?'

'An Army type, that's all I know. Not an officer, probably an NCO.'

'I can see you're pretty hot on Army types as well as accents.'

Isobel laughed. 'Away with you and stop being cheeky!'

As he was walking towards his car she called out after him: 'Drop in again if you're up this way. There's all that whisky to be finished.'

CHAPTER FIVE

The distillery lay in a hollow opposite Letterewe at the foot of Slioch, the mountain standing above Loch Maree on its western shore. A small cluster of white buildings, recognizable as a distillery by the pagoda roofs of the malt kilns, was surrounded by the cottages in which the workers lived, making a village as remote and lonely as any in the Highlands.

Although he had known there was a distillery not far from Loch Maree and from time to time had drunk the malt whisky it produced, Ian had never visited it, nor did he know anyone associated with the company which owned it. Now suddenly it appeared to be obtruding more and more into his life. First he had found the illustrated brochure describing the distillery in his father's tuck-box, then Loch Maree whisky had been served at the golf club dinner and Sandy Ballantine had taken a bottle of it with him to Isobel Gillespies's cottage. Finally that morning he had unexpectedly had a telephone call from Donald Buchanan, the managing director of the West Highland Scotch Whisky Company which owned the distillery and one other.

Ian knew nothing about Donald Buchanan except that he was the younger son of the Prime Minister, Alisdair Buchanan. Donald would be a few years older than Ian, perhaps in his late thirties. Neither Donald nor his elder brother Archie had ever taken any part in politics and it was not surprising that he should be in the whisky business, even though his family had been associated with the steel industry for several generations. With the steel industry in Scotland now moribund, young men of talent and ambition had to look elsewhere for a career, and over the past forty years distilling and exporting whisky had grown into one of the most important commercial activities in the country.

That morning when introducing himself over the telephone, Donald Buchanan had told Ian that he had hoped to have met him at the Invermuir Golf Club dinner, but there had been too many people to speak to and time had run out before they could get together.

'At least I had the chance to enjoy your whisky,' Ian had remarked.

'If you come up to the distillery today, we'll see that you enjoy some more.'

Buchanan had gone on to explain that he had been planning to make an appointment to see Ian at his office on a business matter, the next time he came to Edinburgh. 'But when I heard that you were to be at home for a few days,' he had added, 'I wondered whether we might meet here.'

'I don't see why not.'

'It'll save the expense of a journey to Edinburgh. We're just a small family business, you understand.'

Ian had recognized that as a joke and a very Scottish one. He knew a man who owned one of the largest and most successful food-manufacturing companies in Scotland and who habitually described himself as 'just a small family grocer'. Sometimes light-hearted self-deprecation could be a mask for thriftiness.

He would have liked to have found out more about the West Highland Scotch Whisky Company, about the size of its operations and its standing in the whisky industry, as he always did before meeting a prospective client. Even if there had been time to do so, he would not have found the resources for that kind of information in Invermuir. In any case he had no reason to believe that Donald Buchanan wished to put any business his way. He may have only been looking for some general financial advice.

The distillery, when he reached it, gave the impression of being well managed. The buildings were clean, the roads in good repair, and there were freshly painted signs directing visitors to the distillery offices, the Excise Office, and the warehouses in which the whisky was left to mature. Ian was glad to see peat smoke coming out of the chimneys of the malt kilns, a sign that the distillery still made its own malt. Less than a dozen of the hundred-odd distilleries in Scotland now had their own maltings, preferring to buy it from the large mechanical maltings or professional maltsters. Traditional floor maltings were disappearing and with them part of the ancient craft of making whisky.

As soon as he had parked his car near the offices, a man came out of the entrance to greet him. Donald Buchanan had sandy hair and the complexion of one who spent a good deal of his time out of doors. He was wearing a green tweed suit and carried a deerstalker hat in one hand.

'So kind of you to come all this way,' he said to Ian after introducing himself. 'I'm obliged to you.'

He led Ian into the building and into a room which, one guessed, must be the managing director's office. The furniture was solid and dark and may well have been there since the distillery was built just under a hundred years previously. Half a dozen whisky sample bottles stood on a table in one corner with, in front of them, nosing glasses, some of which had whisky in them. The aroma of malt whisky hung in the air, strong enough to mask the smell of furniture polish. A portrait in oils of a man in Victorian clothes hung in a position of honour facing the door. The expression on the man's face was not one of the patriarchal solemnity usually to be found in portraits hanging in board rooms or offices. Instead one could see a slight smile on the man's lips, a gleam of humour in his eyes. The leisurely business of distilling and the product of the stills, Ian decided, must be reflected in the temperaments of those who owned or managed distilleries, making them more relaxed than the iron-masters and shipbuilders of old.

'Is that one of your forebears?' Ian asked Buchanan, pointing towards the portrait.

'Heavens no! That's old Charlie Macpherson who built this distillery. We Buchanans only became involved when my grandfather was persuaded to buy shares in the company and take a seat on the board. Then eventually the Macphersons sold their interest to our family.'

The distillery clerkess, a stout girl in a flowered dress, brought in coffee and biscuits for them. As he began pouring the coffee, Buchanan said, 'We can have a dram later.'

'That was a fine drop of whisky you provided for the golf club dinner.'

'Yes, it was a bit special; a fifteen-year-old matured in sherry wood.'

'I was told in Edinburgh that you were no longer bottling Loch Maree as a single malt.'

Buchanan sighed in exasperation and raised his eyebrows. 'How do these myths get around? Almost the reverse is true. We have cut down drastically on the whisky we supply to the blending companies, both here and at Glen Torridon, our other distillery.'

'Why is that?'

'Simple economics, old chap. We make more money by selling single malts.'

He told Ian that over the last two or three years single malt whisky had really taken off. Sales had more than doubled in Britain during that time, but the real boom was in exports. Everyone was switching from blended Scotch to malt whisky; in the States, France, Japan, Spain, even in the Middle East. Both of the distilleries belonging to the West Highland Scotch Whisky Company were working to capacity and almost all the whisky they were distilling was laid down to mature to be sold as single malts.

'It's wonderful for Scotland,' Buchanan concluded. 'People are beginning at last to return to the true whisky; malt whisky, the

71

traditional drink of the Highland Scot.'

'That must be good for your company as well.'

'It is, it is. And for most malt whisky distilleries. That is one of the reasons I wished to have a chat with you. At our last board meeting it was suggested that you might be able to help us. They tell me you're a money broker.'

'Our firm is, yes.'

'I suppose you play the same role as a whisky broker?'

'Much the same.'

Ian knew that Buchanan would have dealings from time to time with whisky brokers, even though their function would have greater relevance to companies producing and selling blended whisky. All internationally known Scotches—Johnnie Walker, Dewars, the Famous Grouse—were blends, made up of anything between fifteen and fifty single whiskies from different distilleries, mixed to the proportions of an established formula. All Scotch had to be matured for at least three years and blenders would therefore have to lay down stocks of new whisky in advance of what they forecast their requirements would be. Often a company might find itself short of a particular single whisky which it needed for its blend. In that case it would then go to a whisky broker, who would know where that whisky might be obtained and who would buy it for the company on commission. In the same way, if a blending company had surplus stocks of whisky, a broker would be able to sell them for it.

'Because of the boom in demand for malt whisky,' Buchanan said, 'it looks as though our accounts are likely to have a very substantial surplus at the end of our financial year. We would not wish that money to be standing idle.'

'Could you not use it to lay down more stocks of whisky to meet future increases in sales?'

'That's a shrewd question. I can see you're beginning to understand the whisky business. But no; as I said, both our distilleries are already working to capacity.'

'Then could you not increase the capacity by installing more stills?'

'No. You see our water supply is fully stretched. As it is, in a dry summer we are often obliged to stop distilling through a shortage of water.'

Every malt whisky distillery in Scotland, Ian knew, had its own supply of water, usually a nearby burn or spring. The water was a key factor in determining the flavour and character of the whisky. If the distiller were to use water from a different source, even from another burn on the same hills, the whisky would be different. Since the whole art of running a distillery was to produce a whisky that was always consistent and could be recognized by its flavour, this would not be feasible.

'So we are thinking of placing any surplus funds where they will earn a good interest, but in a relatively short-term investment,' Buchanan continued. 'This will give us time to consider other options; buying another distillery, for example, should one become available.'

'If that's what you wish,' Ian said, 'we would certainly be able to help, but you should be aware that there would be risks.'

'Of course!' Buchanan smiled. 'I'm a simpleton when it comes to finance, but even I know what happened to that Western Isles Council which invested in that Arab bank. At this moment our auditors are preparing our annual accounts. When they have finished and we know what amount of cash is available, you and I can meet again.'

'Who are your auditors?'

'Finlays in Dundee. A good firm. A bit lacking in imagination, but sound.'

Since they had carried their business discussion as far as they could for the present, Buchanan offered to show Ian round the distillery. Ian accepted the offer, for he had only once visited a distillery before and wished to get a better insight into the size and operations of the company.

They made the tour following the chronological sequence of the distilling operations, starting at the point where the barley was delivered. They only used Scottish barley, Buchanan assured Ian. After being steeped in water, the barley was spread out over the malting floor, where it would start to germinate. They saw the maltmen turning it with their sheils—large flat wooden shovels—to control the rate of germination. In the malt kiln the green malt, as it was called, would then be dried by smoke rising from a fire on which peat was burned, which would give the whisky its characteristic smoky flavour.

Much of the distillery's equipment seemed to be new; the mash tun in which the malt, after being ground in a mill, was mixed with hot water to extract the fermentable sugar, and the washbacks, huge wooden cylindrical vessels in which the mash was fermented by the addition of yeast. So were the four gleaming copper stills in which the fermented liquid was distilled twice. Two of the long low traditional warehouses in which the casks of new whisky were left to mature were opened for Ian and Buchanan to inspect. In one of them the casks, stacked three high on top of each other and stretching back into the darkness, had the names of whisky companies stencilled on them; John Walker and Sons, Matthew

Gloag and Son, Charles Mackinlay and Company. These were the blending companies, Buchanan explained, for whom the whisky had been distilled. All the whisky in the other warehouse belonged to the West Highland Scotch Whisky Company, and when matured it would all be bottled as Loch Maree single-malt whisky.

'As you can see,' Buchanan told Ian, 'all the casks belonging to the blending companies were filled some years ago. We're not accepting any orders from them now.'

After the tour they returned to Buchanan's office and he poured two whiskies from a decanter which he took from a cupboard opposite his desk. The whisky was a deep amber colour, showing that it had been matured in a cask which had previously held sherry. Ian had always preferred the full-bodied, rich flavour of Scotch from sherry wood and found the pale whiskies that some companies were producing bland and uninteresting.

'Which of your directors suggested that you might speak to our firm about investment?' he asked Buchanan.

'Our Chairman, General Ballantine.' Buchanan paused and then he added, 'You heard about his death, I suppose?'

'Yes, I read about it.'

'Dreadful business, dreadful! It means a great loss to our company. I don't know how we will ever replace him.'

'Do you really believe it was the IRA who murdered him?'

'Who else could it have been? Did you know Sandy well?'

'Not really. He came to our house in Edinburgh once or twice when I was a lad, that's all.'

While he was speaking, the telephone on Buchanan's desk rang. As he picked it up Ian rose to leave the room, thinking that the call might be private, but Buchanan motioned at him to stay where he was.

The conversation was brief. After listening to the caller, Buchanan said, 'No, I don't think that's a good idea. Not at this stage anyway.' The caller must have argued and Buchanan seemed to be losing patience. Presently he said, 'Then ask Ferret for his opinion. I'll be happy to go along with whatever he advises.'

After ringing off, he turned to Ian. 'Your father will have been devastated by Sandy's murder. I know they were good friends.'

'They were; since their schooldays.'

'I know. We must not mourn Sandy, though. He'd not have liked us to. We'll just drink to the memory of a great man and a good friend.'

Buchanan lifted his glass solemnly and Ian felt he should do the same. When he left the distillery a short time later, he did not go straight home, but drove to Dingwall. For a town of its size, Dingwall had an excellent public library and there he found, as he had expected he would, a copy of *Who's Who*. The entry for General Alexander Ballantine gave details of his birth, education, and marriage, as well as of his military career. He had served in Malaya, Cyprus, and Korea, had spent a spell as an instructor at the Staff College in Camberley, and done a tour as Military Attaché in Washington. For three years he had been GOC Scotland and Governor of Edinburgh Castle. Since leaving the Army he had joined the board of the West Highland Scotch Whisky Company and was also a director of the Tayside Rope Company. Two years previously he became President of the Royal British Legion, Scotland, and was also President of the Scottish Soldiers Resettlement Association.

While he was driving home, Ian wondered why the General had advised the board of the whisky company to consult his firm. Several other firms of money brokers in Edinburgh or in London would have been able to advise Donald Buchanan. Ballantine may only have wished to do the son of his lifelong friend a favour by putting business in his way, but if so it was strange that he had not told Andrew Blackie what he had done.

He realized now that whether or not his father's relationship with Ballantine had been a homosexual one no longer seemed important. On balance he thought it unlikely but it was also irrelevant. Their secret plotting, codewords, and recorded messages, which he had at first thought juvenile, were seeming more sinister now that the IRA appeared to be involved.

When he reached home, he telephoned his office in Edinburgh. Rosemary, his secretary, was a bright girl who had taken a degree in law at university but had not yet managed to find work in the legal profession. She quickly brought him up to date with the current work of the firm, giving him a faint impression that in his absence he was not being missed. To show that he had not completely forgotten business, he asked her to get as much information as she could from the Company Register about the West Highland Scotch Whisky Company, including a copy of its last published accounts. Then, on an impulse, he asked her to do the same for the Tayside Rope Company.

As he was finishing the call, his mother returned home. He heard a car draw up in front of the house, drop her off, and drive away. That morning she had been to a meeting of a local ladies' charity committee and Ian supposed that one of the other members had driven her home.

'How was the meeting?' he asked her when

she came into the room.

'Very professional. Monica MacBain is the chairman and she didn't take long over the agenda, so we girls had time for a lovely gossip afterwards.'

As long as her husband was alive, Fiona Blackie had chosen not to become involved in community activities. That might have been because, not being a local girl, she may have felt that the ladies of Invermuir would not welcome her, or simply that she preferred to devote all her time to her husband. Ian was glad that she now seemed ready to take a greater interest in the life of the small town, for it would be a way of filling her time.

'Be careful!' he teased her, 'The Black Widow will have you drafted into her disciplined corps of do-gooders.'

'I'll not mind if she does,' his mother replied. 'They are such nice people. And you really must not call Monica by that dreadful name. One day you'll forget and call her that to her face.'

'One day! One day! That's what you used to say to me when I was young. "Stop pulling faces, Ian. One day the wind will change and your face will be stuck like that for ever."'

'You're incorrigible! And you must watch your tongue this evening. We're invited to have dinner with Monica and Nick.'

'Tonight? That's very short notice; indecently short.'

'The invitation was made very much on the spur of the moment.'

Mrs Blackie explained that the committee meeting had been held in the MacBain's home. After it was over and the ladies were chatting, MacBain had returned having finished his morning surgery. He had chatted for a while with Mrs Blackie and had asked her how Ian had been getting on with settling his father's affairs.

'Then suddenly, without warning, he suggested that you and I should have dinner with them. Monica didn't seem best pleased until he said we would dine out.'

Ian had no particular wish to spend the evening with the MacBains, but he did not mind if it were to be part of his mother's rehabilitation. 'Where will we dine?' he asked her.

'At Grudie Lodge. It's that country house which has been converted into a hotel. People say that the food is outstanding.'

'It'll be a Scottish chef's idea of nouvelle cuisine. God help us!' Ian said. 'You'd best have some sandwiches ready for a late supper when we get home.'

'Nick is inviting another couple who are new to the town and who he feels we might like to meet.'

'Who's paying?'

'He is of course. So don't be ungrateful.'

Realizing that it was time for the midday news, Mrs Blackie crossed the room and turned on the radio. The announcer had already begun reading and was informing any Scot who might care to listen that the government at Westminster had survived a vote of no confidence. Then he switched to a news item of more interest to Scotland.

'Last night outside Stranraer police shot and killed a man suspected of being an IRA terrorist. The man was driving a van and police believe that he had crossed to Scotland on the ferry from Belfast to fetch a consignment of weapons stolen from an Army barracks. The man has been named as Sean Deeney of the Provisional IRA.'

CHAPTER SIX

Next morning, with the help of Jamie the gardener, Ian brought his father's trunk down from the attic. The ladies' committee, of which Mrs Blackie was now a member, had welcomed the gift of the trunk and its contents which would be sold in the charity shop which they ran in Invermuir. The husband of one of the members had volunteered to collect it that morning and take it in a van to the shop.

When the trunk was standing in the front hall of the house ready to be collected, Ian returned to the attic. He had told his mother that she should not give the tuck-box away as well as the trunk. One reason was that most of what it contained was unsaleable; another was that the events of the past few days had fired his curiosity and he wanted to know whether his father's suspicions about General Ballantine's death were justified. Clearly the two men had been involved in some form of intrigue or plot and there was no safe in the house, nor anywhere else, in which evidence of their secret might have been hidden other than the padlocked tuck-box.

Opening it, he spread the contents on the attic floor. Putting the press cuttings which dealt with Ballantine's career and achievements on one side, he read all those about his death and the obituaries for a second time, but this time more carefully. Only one of them caught his attention. This was an announcement that a memorial service was to be held for the General in St Giles' Cathedral, Edinburgh, at which the address was to be given by his nephew, David Roxburgh QC. Roxburgh, Ian knew, had first become celebrated in Scotland for the brilliance with which he had defended a number of Scottish nationalists when they had appeared in court charged with terrorism. The press cutting was not dated, so Ian could not tell whether the memorial service had already been held.

Nothing else in the tuck-box seemed to be of sufficient consequence to have been kept locked away. The brochure of the West Highland Scotch Whisky Company was no more than a piece of publicity designed to be handed out to visitors at the distilleries, and he could not see how it could have any relevance to the death of General Ballantine. The posters were only of historical interest now, for the Scottish nationalist bodies which had published them were now defunct; sunk or scuttled by frustration or ineptitude.

The four books which had been kept in the box also seemed innocent enough. The edition of *A Grandfather's Tales* was older than Ian had at first thought, published in 1923, and its pages were dog-eared. Ian glanced through it looking for the important landmarks in Scotland's history and was amused to see how Scott had romanticized them. He hunted for 1320, the date of the Declaration of Arbroath, and found it, with difficulty for some of the pages of the book were missing. Both of the books on climbing, Ian decided, must have found their way into the tuck-box by mistake and should have been in the trunk, together with the other souvenirs of his father's hobbies. The one which named and described all the mountains over three thousand feet in Scotland, popularly known as Munros, had a list of them in order of height, and Ian noticed that his father had put a tick against some of them, presumably those he had climbed at one time or another.

The copy of *Inglorious Failure* interested him because of the comments which his father had scribbled in the margins of the pages, but he could not see how any of the books could in any way be connected with the murder of General Ballantine at Ardnadaig.

He looked into the box again in case there might be something at the bottom which he had overlooked, perhaps another microcassette for the tape-recorder. All he could see was a rectangular slip of white paper on which were printed the words 'With the Compliments of the Scotch Whisky Association' and underneath an address in Edinburgh. For a moment he was puzzled, then he remembered that when he had first opened the box he had found among all the other books and pamphlets a purple booklet, an *Annual Statistical Report* published by the Scotch Whisky Association. Now it was not there, nor was it among the other publications which he had spread out on the floor. Another thing which was missing was the Ordnance Survey map of

Perthshire.

Ian could think of no explanation for their disappearance. His mother would not have come up into the attic, and even if she had she would not have opened the tuck-box and taken away a booklet and a map which could have no possible interest for her. He began to wonder whether in fact he had seen them there or whether it had been some trick of his memory or imagination. Finally he decided he should not be wasting time worrying about anything so trivial, so he returned everything to the box, with the exception of the copy of *Inglorious Failure*, which he took downstairs with him.

While he waited for the van which was to collect the trunk, he began reading the book. He had read it once when it was first published, but had forgotten its mood of bitter pessimism. The author had been one of the leaders of the Scottish nationalist movement in the early days when it had seemed that nothing could deflect it from its triumphant progress towards independence which reached its peak in 1968, when the Scottish Nationalist Party had obtained the largest share of the votes cast in the municipal elections.

Since that time, the author claimed, there had been only decline as the movement for independence was gradually eroded by its own divisions. There had been a proliferation of splinter groups, the 1320 Club, Siol Nan Gaidheal, the Scottish Workers' Republic, the Scottish National Liberation Army, and several others. Some were led by intellectuals who occupied themselves planning strategies for the day when independence came. Others were formed by agitators, who believed that only violence would compel a Westminster parliament to set Scotland free. Scornfully the author described the petty acts of 'tartan terrorism', the blowing up of letterboxes and electricity pylons and sections of oil-piping. Plans to seize small Scottish towns to spark off a national uprising had never materialized, but there had been raids on banks and post offices, carried out to raise funds for republican movements. The comments which Andrew Blackie had written in the margins of this section of the book showed that he had shared the author's contempt for these trivial heroics.

Ian's reading was interrupted by the arrival of the van which was to pick up the trunk and the two suitcases into which his mother had packed his father's clothes that were also to be given to charity. When he went outside, he saw that it was not only the van that was standing outside the house. Behind it, climbing out of her small car, was Mrs MacBain.

'I decided that I should come along, to

make sure that old Murdo collected the right things,' she told Ian, nodding in the direction of the man driving the van. 'It's extremely kind of your mother to give so many clothes.'

Monica MacBain was tall and slender, with a head that was made to look even smaller than it was by her cropped hair. Everything about her was black; her hair, her clothes, her shoes and her large black eyes. Although she had a reputation for being kind and spent much of her time working for charitable enterprises, her manner was one of humourless severity. One had the impression that she believed that most people—and all men—were bumbling incompetents and it was her task in life to make up for their shortcomings.

She watched as Ian and Murdo loaded the trunk and the suitcases into the van. 'Was there not something more to be taken?' she asked. 'A box?'

'No. There is a box in which my father kept souvenirs of his schooldays and his youth, but these have only sentimental value and we decided to keep them, for the present at least.'

'Of course. I understand.'

As they were talking, Mrs Blackie, who had been in one of the upstairs rooms when the van arrived, came out of the house to join them. The three of them chatted for a while as they watched the van drive away and then Mrs MacBain left as well.

After she had gone Mrs Blackie said to Ian, 'I told Monica quite distinctly yesterday that you wished to keep your father's tuck-box, for the time being at least.'

'She must have forgotten.'

'I have noticed that she is becoming quite forgetful. Do you suppose it might be the first symptoms of Alzheimer's disease?'

'I'm sure it isn't.'

Ian found it difficult to restrain a smile. In his opinion Monica MacBain was too alert to forget anything which it would be to her advantage to remember. What amused him was that his mother should be concerned about Monica's lapse of memory, for she was herself becoming increasingly absent-minded. It was only the absent-mindedness of age though, caused by lack of concentration, and he was sure that there was no cause for alarm over her health.

As they returned to the house, the telephone rang and when Ian picked it up he heard a girl's voice which he did not recognize. 'Is that Ian Blackie? This is Isobel.'

It took a moment for him to realize that Isobel must be Isobel Gillespie, the writer. 'Hullo. How are you?'

'Are you very busy?' she asked. 'What I mean is would you be able to come up here today?'

'Why? Are you having difficulty finishing that whisky?'

'No. I'm being serious.'

Ian could sense an awkwardness in her words and regretted his flippancy. 'Would you like me to come now?'

'If it's not too inconvenient.'

'I've a couple of phone calls to make and then I'll leave.' Something in her tone worried him, so he added, 'Is anything wrong?'

'We can talk about it when you arrive. I'll be waiting for you in the inn along the road from my place.'

She put the phone down, leaving Ian wondering what might have possibly happened to provoke her request. He had formed the impression that she was a self-reliant person, proud of her independence and not likely to ask favours lightly from a comparative stranger.

He made one, not two, telephone calls, to his office in Edinburgh, and was assured that nothing had happened in the past twenty-four hours that demanded his attention. His secretary told him that as soon as she had copies of the report and accounts of the West Highland Scotch Whisky Company and the Tayside Rope Company she would fax them to him, using a service which an enterprising newsagent in

Invermuir had recently made available to its customers. Then, having told his mother that he would not be lunching at home, he set out in his car for Shieldaig.

The day was soft, with a mist lying on the hills and a hint of impending rain which, from his knowledge of Wester Ross, Ian was confident would remain no more than a hint. When rain fell in that part of the country, there was no mistaking it. The loveliness of Loch Maree, even in the sombre light, was enough to distract his thoughts from curiosity and he stopped wondering what Isobel had to tell him that could not have been told over the telephone. He drove at a leisurely pace, with no sense of urgency and was pleased that already, after only a few days, he was becoming attuned to the pace of life in the western Highlands.

Isobel was waiting for him in the bar at the inn. Apart from an anorak over her shoulders, she was wearing much the same kind of loose, floppy dress as she had been at their last meeting, but looked untidier, almost dishevelled. She was holding a half-empty cup of coffee and Ian noticed that her hands were grimy.

'I feel terrible, dragging you all the way up here.'

She seemed calm enough, but the composure, the good-humoured tolerance which had made such an impression on him when they first met had vanished. Instead he could see uneasiness in her eyes, an anxiety which was not all that far from panic.

'What's happened?' he asked and without thinking took her hands in his protectively.

'Last night my cottage was burnt down.'

'Good God! How?'

'The firemen think it was arson; a petrol bomb.'

★   ★   ★

'In a way it was my fault,' Isobel said.

'What are you saying?'

They had moved from the bar counter to a table in a corner of the room. Ian had bought a whisky for her and one for himself. Isobel looked as though she needed a drink. There was no one else in the bar at that time of the morning so they could talk freely.

'I was not honest with you. When you asked me if Sandy had left anything at my cottage when he went to Ardnadaig, I avoided answering the question.'

'So he did leave something?'

'Yes, a leather briefcase with some papers in it. They must have been important, for Sandy phoned me when he reached Ardnadaig and found that he had forgotten it. He asked me to keep it safe till he got back, to hide it.'

As he realized the implications of what she

was telling him, Ian stared at her in astonishment. 'And you are suggesting that your house was burned down simply to destroy those papers? I can't believe it!'

Isobel ignored his protests. 'The reason I didn't tell you about the briefcase before was that I didn't trust you. I'm sorry. But that other man had come and asked the same question.'

'I can understand your not wishing to tell me, but why should anyone burn the house down? Why did they not just break in and steal the papers?'

'Maybe because whoever it was couldn't find the briefcase. On two occasions recently I have had the feeling that someone has come and searched the cottage when I was out.'

'Broken into the place?'

'No. We never lock doors around here.'

'Then what makes you believe the cottage was searched?'

'There are always small things which tell one. A vase has been moved, a cushion put back in a slightly different place.'

'But nothing was taken?'

'Nothing. I had the briefcase well hidden.'

'That still doesn't explain why they set light to your cottage. They could have come and searched again.'

'Yes, I've wondered about that. Perhaps time was running out and the papers could not be allowed to fall into the wrong hands. They were too important.'

'Or too incriminating. Where were you when the fire was started?'

'Here in the inn, having a drink.'

She explained that the previous evening, after having her supper, she had come round to the inn as she often did. The walk and a few minutes spent chatting with local people made a break in an evening which was otherwise spent working on a book. While she was in the inn a neighbour had rushed in to tell her that the cottage was on fire. He had seen the flames while on his way home from Shieldaig. Everyone in the inn had hurried with her to the cottage, but when they reached it the fire was too advanced, the flames too fierce, to allow any attempt to salvage any of her belongings. By the time the fire brigade had arrived, only the shell of the cottage remained.

'So you've lost everything?'

'It appears that way. The place is still smouldering, so the firemen told me to go back this afternoon and they will help to see if anything can be salvaged.'

'Have you any idea of who might have started the fire?'

'The neighbour who raised the alarm says he saw a man driving away in the direction of Shieldaig. It can't have been anyone local and by the description of the car it could well be the same man who came here after Sandy's death.'

'The bogus chauffeur?'

'It seems like it.'

Ian shook his head in disbelief. 'This is appalling! I feel responsible for dragging you into this.'

'Don't be absurd. The bogus chauffeur, as you call him, came to question me before you did. Remember?'

'I suspect that it must be the same man who went to Ardnadaig in the afternoon after Sandy was killed. He searched his room at the Ferry Inn as well.'

'What does it all mean?' Isobel demanded. 'Bombs, attempted burglary, arson! How have you and I become involved in this and who is behind it?'

Ian did not reply to her question, although he might have attempted a speculative answer. Nothing he could say would console or comfort her for the horror she had endured and his feeling of guilt for what had happened still persisted.

'We can talk about that later,' he told her. 'Much more important is what will you do now? Where did you spend last night?'

'A large part of the night was taken up watching the firemen trying to put the blaze out. Then my neighbours took me home and insisted that I go to bed. Everyone has been so kind.'

'Have you lost everything? All your clothes?'

'I suppose I have, but clothes can easily be replaced and everything in the cottage was insured. What is irreplaceable is all I had written of a new book that I have been working on.'

'So you'll have to start it again?'

Isobel must have felt that he did not really appreciate the extent of the loss she had suffered, for she said indignantly, 'You can't possibly know what that means to a writer, how much work goes into writing a book. The idea, the plot, planning the story are relatively easy and painless. The writing itself is the real labour, choosing the words, composing the sentences, striking the right balance between description and narrative and dialogue to sustain the reader's interest. That takes time; time and self-discipline.'

'I'm sure it does. I was not being unsympathetic.'

'I have always had a dread of losing what I have written or having it destroyed by accident. It is almost a phobia. I make copies of everything and keep the copies in separate rooms; sometimes when I'm in Edinburgh in separate houses.'

'You write using a word processor, do you not?'

'I do. And mine was destroyed in the fire, together with all the discs, all the copies.'

'That's dreadful!' A plan was beginning to form in Ian's mind. He told Isobel, 'You can't stay here. You'll be needing to buy new clothes, to find another word processor, buy paper.'

'There are shops in Gairloch.'

'You must be joking!' Ian had been to Gairloch and knew that it had not more than half a dozen shops, none of which sold ladies' clothes. 'Look, I'm ravenous. See if you can order us some sandwiches, while I go and make a phone call.'

The call he made from a phone box outside the inn took longer than he had expected, because he ran out of change and had to fetch more. When he returned to the bar two plates of sandwiches and coffee stood on the table.

'Everything's arranged,' he told Isobel. 'We'll spend the afternoon seeing what we can salvage from the fire and then you'll come to stay with my mother and me in Invermuir.'

'I'll do no such thing.'

She had to be convinced by reasoning that what he had suggested was the only sensible course. In Invermuir she would be able to buy what she needed to tide her over the emergency and they would be able to drive up to Shieldaig, every day if that were needed, to deal with the aftermath of the fire. From Invermuir, too, she could more easily contact her insurers, her solicitor, and her bank.

They spent a depressing afternoon with the firemen and helpful neighbours, picking among the charred debris at the bottom of the cottage. The frame of the house, solidly built from stone, was intact, and, everyone agreed, it could be restored for use without too much difficulty. Ian could see though, that Isobel was upset as they found the remains of her possessions, charred books, ornaments twisted into shapelessness, fragments of fabric.

When they had done all they could and the time came for them to leave for Invermuir, her spirits seemed to lift and she became almost cheerful. Ian admired her resilience. When they drove off in his car, watched by the crofters and the firemen, she laughed.

'That's my reputation down the tubes!' she said.

'What do you mean?'

'What must my neighbours be thinking as they watch me being carried off—and by a man?'

On the way to Invermuir they talked of practical matters; how soon the insurance company could be persuaded to have the cottage inspected, whether there were architects locally who could supervise its restoration, and, most important of all, how soon she would be able to find a word processor and start work on her book. Even as they talked Ian could not help thinking of the danger to which she had been exposed.

She may have guessed what he was thinking, for suddenly she said, 'Do you suppose the petrol bomb would have been thrown into the cottage if I had been inside?'

'One likes to hope not, but whoever is behind all this seems completely ruthless. Anyway Sandy's papers are destroyed now, so maybe that'll be an end to the matter.'

'Not necessarily. I made a copy of them.'

'Good God! Why?'

'I was ashamed at the way I had behaved, so I thought I'd make a copy and send it to you. I had just finished it when I left for the inn last evening.'

'Surely the copy must have been burnt in the fire as well?'

'No. I put what I found in the papers on to my WPC, meaning to run it off on the printer this morning.'

'But the word processor was destroyed.'

'Yes, but for some reason, I don't know why, I slipped the disc into my pocket.' She took a disc in its small plastic box from the pocket of her anorak and gave it to Ian.

CHAPTER SEVEN

'She's a remarkable girl,' Mrs Blackie commented to Ian.

They were having breakfast together the following morning; just the two of them, for Mrs Blackie had insisted on taking a breakfast tray up to Isobel in the room where she had spent the night. She told Ian how, when she had arrived there, she had found Isobel already out of bed and writing. The children's story on which she had been working in Shieldaig had to be rewritten, so she had already started on it, writing in longhand as there was no word processor in the house.

'People say that self-discipline is important for a writer,' Ian replied. 'More important than talent. Though I've no doubt that Isobel has talent as well.'

'Poor wee soul! All her clothes, her jewellery, her books, have gone. She has nothing left.'

'I know. And yet she's so calm. Her equanimity is astonishing.'

'You may think that, but she was crying in the night. I woke and could hear her sobbing. I so wanted to go and comfort her.'

Ian found the thought of Isobel lying sobbing in the darkness strangely moving, even though in retrospect he knew he should not be surprised after what the girl had been through. To mask his own emotion, he said to his mother jokingly, 'It was probably your kindness that made her cry.'

'What nonsense! How can you say such a thing?'

Ian knew that when they had arrived at Invermuir the previous evening, Isobel had been surprised and grateful for what Mrs Blackie had already done for her. Ian too had been surprised by his mother's resourcefulness. When he had telephoned from Shieldaig to say that he would be bringing Isobel to stay with them, she had questioned him about her build, her complexion, the colour of her hair. So when they arrived home a room was ready for Isobel, with the bed made, flowers, even an electric blanket and, in the bathroom, shampoo, bath oil, toothbrushes and toothpaste. Laid out on the bed were a pair of slacks and a sweater, a skirt, and a jumper.

When Isobel had tried to thank her, Mrs Blackie had cut short her protests. 'It's nothing; nothing at all. You'll not be wanting to buy clothes here in Invermuir, so I just took these from the charity shop in the town. They'll do till you can buy something better. When you've finished with them, we'll have them cleaned and take them back to the shop. Monica MacBain would not even let me pay for them.'

If Isobel had been amused, as Ian was, by his mother's typical thriftiness, she had not shown it. She had bathed and changed into the slacks and sweater and the three of them had spent the evening quietly, without ever talking of the fire or speculating on how it had been started. Now, in the morning, he was wondering whether she might show any delayed effects of the shock she must have suffered. The feeling that he had unwittingly been responsible for exposing her to dangers which, even now, she did not fully appreciate, still persisted.

'What will the poor lass do now?' his mother asked.

'She'll need to contact her insurers first and then a firm of architects about rebuilding the cottage. And her solicitors as well, no doubt.'

'How typical of a man!' his mother exclaimed. 'To think first of practical issues. I was talking of clothes. Isobel will not be wanting to buy anything in Invermuir.'

Ian smiled, remembering how when he had first met Isobel he had wondered whether she might be wearing clothes handed down to her by an older woman. In his opinion she looked better in the clothes his mother had brought home from the charity shop than in the dress she had worn in Shieldaig, but he knew his mother would not be pleased if he were to say so.

'No. Once the matter of the cottage is settled, I'll drive her down to Edinburgh.'

'You'll make sure she's not short of money, will you not.'

'Of course.'

'You're a good lad, Ian.'

When Isobel came downstairs not long afterwards, one could see no sign of tears or of nerves in her manner. She seemed almost happy, as though beginning to work on her book had revitalized her. The three of them talked about her plans for the day and then she went and spent more than an hour on the telephone. After that she made a list of small personal articles which she needed and which Mrs Blackie would buy for her in Invermuir that day. Finally Ian fetched his car and he and Isobel set out for Shieldaig.

On the way she suddenly asked him, 'What have you done with that floppy disc that I gave you?'

'I have it with me.'

'Did you not think of having it printed out? There must be somewhere in Invermuir where that could be done.'

'I did, but I decided that the fewer people who know about the disc the better.'

'Security, eh? You're taking this whole affair of Sandy's death seriously?'

'We have to.'

Isobel appeared to think about his answer

for a time, as though she had another question for him but was uncertain of how he would respond to it. Finally she said, 'Do you suppose that Sandy might have been working for the intelligence service? That would explain this cloak-and-dagger stuff and the phone call from Northern Ireland.'

'From what I know it seems more likely that he and my father were members of some Scottish Nationalist organization. I find the secrecy puzzling, though. One would have thought that any Scot Nat group would be looking for publicity, if only to attract more support for itself.'

'Sandy would have enjoyed the secrecy, the codewords, having his phone tapped. In many ways he was still a schoolboy. The development of some men seems to be arrested at the point when they leave school.'

'Is that the voice of women's lib?' Ian teased her.

'Not at all. You know it's true.'

Ian knew it was true, for a master at his old school in Edinburgh had been a perfect example of Isobel's theory. The man had been at the school himself, left to go to university in Edinburgh, returned immediately after graduating as a junior master, and stayed there for the whole of his teaching career. Now, approaching retirement, he still had the outlook and the ideas of an eighteen-year-old. Often he would use the same expressions and the same slang that had been the fashion forty years previously. On reflection Ian could see now that his father too, shielded from life in the civil service, had retained many of his boyish habits and his outlook. He remembered the letter from Sandy Ballantine which his father had kept for so many years in his school tuck-box and he could easily imagine how the two men, brought together, might relapse into the attitudes of the adolescence they had shared. The thought made him feel uncomfortable, reminding him of his suspicions about their relationship.

'What was in Sandy's briefcase anyway?' he asked Isobel.

'Sheets of paper. Most of them just covered in numbers and a few scribbles here and there.'

'Oh, no! Don't tell me he was using codes!'

'Probably. You'll see when you have the disc run off on a printer.'

'You were right,' Ian said, giving way to his irritation. 'They were just arrested schoolboys.'

'The codes that amateurs invent are usually easy to crack. I'll show you how.'

When they reached the burnt-out shell of her cottage, they found nobody there, but a note had been fixed to the wall near where the front door had been. It told Isobel that everything salvaged from the fire had been stored in the barn of a neighbouring croft.

'That'll be Angus Macduff's place,' Isobel said. 'But before we go over there, I'll take another look round the cottage.'

They walked in the ruins of the cottage and she pointed out the different rooms, where her writing table had been and her bed and her dressing table and the cupboard in which she had kept her clothes. The old-fashioned iron stove had survived the fire almost unmarked, but the bathroom suite which Isobel had herself installed had evidently been acrylic and must have been one of the first things to burst into flames.

At first Ian had thought that her reason for walking in what was left of her cottage must simply be nostalgia, but he could see no sorrow in her face. She seemed more curious than upset, studying everything she saw carefully, as though she wished to memorize every detail. Was this a writer's habit, he wondered, storing impressions so that one day they could be used in a description of the scene in a book?

When they walked across to the neighbour's croft, they found no one there and the barn, which was not much more than a shed, was locked.

'Did you not tell me that up here people don't lock their doors?' Ian teased Isobel.

'They do when they are looking after the property of other folk. And Angus is from Skye, so he'll be jealous of the reputation that the islanders have.'

'What reputation?'

She told him the story of how on Skye not so many years previously Dunvegan Castle had caught fire. The Macleods, who owned the castle, had fought the fire with the help of scores of local folk, and had been forced to bring their possessions out into the grounds: paintings, silver, armour, and even the legendary Fairy Flag. Scarcely had they done so when heavy rain began to fall, an event not unknown on Skye. Quickly the islanders had carried off everything that might be damaged to the safety of their own homes. When the representatives of the Macleods' insurers arrived at the castle, they were appalled, convinced that many, if not all, of the valuables would never be seen again. They were wrong. On the day when the Macleods were able to re-occupy the castle, crofters from all over the island arrived, on foot, on horseback, in farm carts, vans, and lorries, bringing back what had been in their safekeeping. Every painting, every piece of furniture, every heirloom was returned.

'That's your Highland folk,' Isobel said when her story was finished.

'For a Sassenach you seem to have taken quite a shine to the Highlanders!'

'Listen to him! You're a Sassenach yourself.'

'Not at all. Though I was brought up in Edinburgh, I was born in Invermuir.'

Isobel looked back towards her cottage. 'When my place is rebuilt, I'll have some changes made. It'll need to be more comfortable if I'm to live here for most of the time.'

'What have you in mind?'

'For a start something better than the apology for a bathroom that I had before.'

'You wish to improve the private facilities?' Ian asked her, mimicking the tone and the accent of those Scots who try to appear refined.

'Facilities?'

'That's what they call a bathroom and lavatory in the travel brochures. Tourists today are very demanding. They ask for bedrooms with "private facilities".'

'Mine don't have to be private. Just a touch more luxurious than what I've had up here so far.'

'You Sassenachs are all soft!'

Presently Angus Macduff returned with his handful of sheep that had been grazing on the common land of the township. He was a tall man, with a jaw that might have been carved out of granite, but one could sense that he was also a gentle man and courteous.

'One of the constables from Gairloch was here looking for you, Miss Isobel,' he said as he took the padlock off the door of the barn.

'How long ago?'

'At the back of eleven. He was no best pleased when he learnt that you were away.'

'What did he expect? That I would spend the night in the fields, waiting for the man?'

'He's a poor wee creature and no very perceptive. But then what can one expect when they insist on sending us a constable from Aberdeen and another from Strathclyde?'

'When you've finished here maybe we should go over to Gairloch and see what he wants,' Ian suggested to Isobel.

'I'd not bother to myself,' Macduff said. 'Likely he'll be away to Poolewe by now. While he was here he had a message that there was a bad motor crash near the bridge there this morning.'

He left them in the barn looking at what little remained of Isobel's furniture and personal possessions. Much of it need never have been salvaged, for it was clearly unusable. Only a sewing machine had escaped the flames unscathed.

'Sod's law!' Isobel commented. 'If I had to lose anything that would have been my first choice. I hate sewing.'

'Is this Sandy's briefcase?' Ian picked a charred piece of leather, still recognizable as a briefcase and with a metal lock on which the initials A.B. had been engraved.

'Yes, but his papers were not in it. I took them out and replaced them with some old notes that I had made for my new book.'

'And you hid his stuff?'

'Yes; rather skilfully I thought. I slipped each sheet into a different file or book. You saw how many books there were in the cottage. It would have taken hours, even days, for anyone to find them.'

Ian smiled. 'You seem to be pretty good at the cloak-and-dagger game yourself.'

'I am. I'd have made a good spy, I believe.'

Ian waited by the door while Isobel toured the barn examining the other items that had been salvaged. She had brought an old envelope and a pencil with her and began jotting down a note from time to time. He wondered whether she would ever have made an inventory of what was in her cottage; if not she was likely to have problems with her insurers.

He was still holding the remains of the briefcase and, noticing that its flap had not been fastened, he glanced inside and saw some fragments of the sheets of paper that Isobel had put in it. Most of them were no more than scraps and so discoloured that one could not tell whether anything had been typed or written on them. One portion of a sheet, larger than the rest, had been scorched grey rather than brown and Ian could see on it the words and numbers of what might have been a table or list. He could just make out the heading above them.

FLASH POINTS OF LIQUIDS

He tried to separate the fragment from the other scraps, so that he could read what was under the heading, but as soon as he held it between his fingers it crumbled into ashes.

CHAPTER EIGHT

In the inn, after leaving Macduff's barn, Isobel said to Ian, 'I wonder whether the man who claimed to be Sandy's driver really did start the fire.'

'Can you think of anyone else who might have done?'

'No. I suppose it must have been him.'

'Would you recognize him if you saw him again?'

'Surely. I can see him now; a typical Scottish soldier; short, thick-set, tough, red hair turning grey, Clydeside accent, a boxer's face. In his fifties, I should think, and probably out of the Army now.'

'Sounds more as if he were just out of Barlinnie.'

'The prison? No, he was too fit for that; the sort of man who runs up mountains.'

'Could you describe his features?'

'I think so.'

'Then hang on a minute.'

Leaving the inn, Ian went out to his car and fetched the small sketch pad which he always carried in the glove compartment. Often when he had to wait for any length of time in the car he would amuse himself by scribbling. Once in an Edinburgh traffic jam he had almost been arrested when a policeman saw him sketching at the wheel.

When he returned to the inn and Isobel saw the pad, she said, 'You're not going to try to draw the man, surely!'

'Why not? I've often thought that I could do those identikit pictures of rapists that they show on television. Now, what shape of head did he have?'

Isobel did her best to describe the man's features, his jaw, chin, nose, forehead, and eyes. As she did so Ian made a sketch of each feature, showed it to her, and then redrew it, changing the outlines until she was satisfied with the resemblance. Gradually a face began to take shape.

'You're on the right lines,' she said. 'At a range of half a mile and in semi-darkness that could be the man.'

'Less of the comedy please! Let's just keep working on it.'

112

Finally, after many of the pad's sheets had been torn up and discarded, he had drawn a face which she admitted was a fair likeness of the man who had claimed to be the General's driver. His most distinctive feature, she told Ian, were his eyebrows, red and bushy, which seemed to protrude out above his eyes, giving him an aggressive, defiant look.

'What are we going to do with this work of art?' she asked.

'Come with me.'

They went to the telephone and dialled the number of the Mrs Smart of Inverness, the photograph of whose self-catering cottage had been marked by Ian's father in the tourist brochure. Mrs Smart told them that the cottage was not rented at that time and that if they wished to see it they could get a key from a Mrs Campbell who lived a mile or two from it. She gave them directions to the cottage and to Mrs Campbell's home.

Leaving the inn they drove there, for most of the journey on the same roads that Ian had followed when he first came to Isobel's cottage. They found the cottage with some difficulty just off a road which was no more than a track, with a fine view of Loch Torridon. Mrs Campbell's croft lay two miles beyond it.

When they explained why they had come, Mrs Campbell handed them the key to the cottage. 'There's everything you'd need there; a stove, pots and pans and plates, and blankets too. You would need to bring your own sheets though, should you decide to rent it.'

'Is it often vacant?' Ian asked.

'Aye, most of the time. The man who rented it last is away now. I was surprised he was satisfied with it. People want something grander these days, television even.'

'And private facilities,' Isobel said, not looking at Ian so that she could keep a straight face.

'Aye, those too. You'll be bringing the key back to me when you've inspected it, will you not?'

The inspection did not take long. The cottage with its two rooms offered only the basic necessities for living there, but it was clean, almost too clean, as though the floors had been scrubbed and every trace of any previous occupation removed.

'This would make an ideal place for anyone who wished to stay near Ardnadaig and remain unnoticed,' Ian remarked.

'You're thinking of the bogus chauffeur. Could he have been sent up here to keep an eye on Sandy? He might have been his minder.'

'Or his murderer. Up here he could have made his bomb undisturbed, taken it across to Ardnadaig by night and placed it on the boat, without too much difficulty. He might even have detonated it by radio from the hill overlooking the loch, as he watched Sandy sail out to sea.'

'And he would have stayed on in the cottage here while he was trying to get his hands on any incriminating papers that Sandy had left behind.'

'Yes. People would think he was on holiday and take no notice of his movements. Then yesterday, after setting light to your place, he would have taken off.'

They returned to Mrs Campbell's croft and handed the key back to her, saying that if they decided to rent the cottage they would telephone Mrs Smart to make the booking.

'You could do worse than take it,' she told them. 'The rent is really low and folk like you would not be worrying about having no television set.'

'The place is beautifully clean,' Isobel told her. 'I suppose you go in and clean after each let.'

'Aye, I do, but there was no need for that this time. Yon fellow Chalmers had left it spotless. Everything scrubbed and he'd even taken his rubbish away with him.'

'You say his name was Chalmers?'

'Aye, Frank Chalmers.'

'What did he look like?' Ian asked.

'Not so tall, but strong. He could look after himself, I should say.'

Ian pulled the sketch he had made from his pocket. 'Could this have been him?'

Mrs Campbell studied the drawing for a time before replying. 'It well might. Those are the man's eyebrows surely and there's a look of him in the eyes as well.' She looked at Ian curiously. 'Are you from the police?'

'We're not,' Isobel replied, 'it's just that this man came to my house in Shieldaig claiming to know my father and we just thought that he might have been staying here.'

'Maybe you're right, but he's away now.'

As they were driving away, heading for Invermuir, Isobel said, 'Did you notice Mrs Campbell taking a long, hard look at my left hand?'

'Your left hand?'

'No wedding ring. She'll be thinking we are looking for two weeks of undisturbed passion, without even a TV to distract us.'

'I hope you were not embarrassed.'

'Embarrassed? Huh! chance would be a fine thing, as they say.'

Ian knew she was laughing at him, but not unkindly. He decided that she probably thought him staid and conventional, stamped in the mould of an Edinburgh upbringing, and would enjoy teasing him. Her own character was beginning to show itself in her tongue-in-cheek remarks.

On the drive to Invermuir her mood

seemed to change. She said to him thoughtfully, 'Your father seems to have been a pretty good sleuth. He found out where Sandy was staying at Ardnadaig and from where he hired that boat.'

'Sandy might well have told him that. In spite of the secrecy they had their own way of communicating.' Ian told her about the recorder and the cassettes.

'Your father also found out about our friend Chalmers, if that's his real name, and that he was staying in the wee cottage.'

'I have the feeling that Chalmers was also involved in whatever weird group Sandy and Dad had formed.'

'But you're saying that even so he murdered Sandy?'

'Yes, but I've no idea why.'

'If Chalmers knew that your father had found that out, then he would also have been in danger.'

'That had struck me.'

'What will you do now?'

Ian had already admitted to himself that he had no idea of what he should do next. The man Chalmers had disappeared and would be difficult, if not impossible, to trace for he had shown himself to be ruthless and resourceful. He had left no evidence to prove his complicity in either General Ballantine's death or in setting fire to Isobel's cottage.

'The copies you made of Sandy's papers

might give us a clue to what we should do next.'

'When will you print out what's on the disc?'

'That would best be done in Edinburgh. The WPC in my flat is the same model as yours was. Why don't we drive down there tomorrow?'

'That would be great! I could buy some clothes and also start reorganizing my life. It would be best if I stayed in Edinburgh while my cottage is being rebuilt. Do you know of any inexpensive hotels there?'

'Why not stay in my flat, at least for the time being?'

'I couldn't possibly do that.'

'Why not? The place is empty and I shall be staying on in Invermuir with my mother for at least another two weeks. That would give you time to make some permanent arrangement.'

'We'll see.'

'When I was a lad my mother would often say that when I asked for something I really wanted or a special treat. I soon learnt that it always meant "no".'

'Well, don't count on that with me,' Isobel replied, and then she added, 'and don't go offering the flat to some other bird!'

At home in Invermuir Ian found a large brown envelope waiting for him. His secretary had gathered most of the information he had wanted about the West Highland Scotch Whisky Company and the Tayside Rope Company. She had faxed everything to the newsagent in Invermuir who had kindly sent a girl assistant round to the house with the faxes. Ian took them up to his bedroom to read.

The accounts of the whisky company, published almost a year previously, were sound without being spectacular, showing a satisfactory operating profit and a dividend which must have pleased the shareholders. The amount of retained profit was not as large as Ian had expected, nor were the company's reserves as shown in the balance sheet, and he could see no reason why it would need the services of a money broker, unless of course the trading profit for the financial year just ending had been substantially greater.

Included in the report and accounts was a list of the directors of the company who had been on the board at the end of the last financial year. From this Ian saw, as he had expected, that General Ballantine had been the chairman and Donald Buchanan the managing director, but he was totally unprepared for the surprise of seeing among the names of the other board members that of Andrew Blackie. He had no idea that his father had joined the board of the whisky company, although there had been no reason, once he had left the civil service, why he should not have done. Nicholas MacBain was also a director and so was David Roxburgh QC, who had been due to give the address at the memorial service to Ballantine.

The report and accounts of the Tayside Rope Company provided more surprises, for both his father and General Ballantine had been directors. The chairman of the company was Tristram Stewart, and Graeme Ross, the former Chief Constable of Tayside Police, was also on the board. A Peter Walker was the managing director.

Ian knew there was no reason why the whisky company and the rope company should not have interlocking directorships. It was not against the law and there might be a financial link as well. Even so, had his father and Ballantine not died before the Invermuir Golf Club dinner, there would have been no less than six directors from the two companies present that evening, one of whom had organized it while two others had made speeches. The arrangement, if not incestuous, was certainly very cosy and Ian distrusted cosiness.

Rosemary had also found out some general information about the Tayside Rope Company and had faxed it to Ian with the accounts. The company had been founded years ago when Dundee was the centre of the jute industry and had always had a sound reputation. In recent years it had diversified and was now engaged in the leisure industry, specializing in the production of equipment for outdoor activities, marquees, flags, tents, sleeping bags, sporting rifles, shot-guns and even climbing boots. It owned a small subsidiary company called 'Endurance Holidays' which arranged camping and climbing package holidays, mainly, but not exclusively, in Scotland.

Included in the faxes which Rosemary had sent him was a photocopy of a press cutting from the *Financial Times*, dated only a week previously. It was from the appointments columns and announced that General Douglass Wreford was to be the chairman of the West Highland Scotch Whisky Company. General Wreford, formerly of the King's Own Scottish Borderers, was also on the board of Peebles Handcraft Woollens Limited and of the Tayside Rope Company.

As Ian went downstairs he wondered why, when he was at Loch Maree distillery, Donald Buchanan had not told him that his father had been a director of the whisky company. It was possible that Buchanan may have assumed that Ian already knew. On the other hand he may have had a motive for concealing the fact.

When his mother met him at the bottom of the stairs, she told him, 'You've been in great demand today, Ian. I've two phone messages for you.'

'From whom?'

'The first was from Tristram Stewart. Your father worked under him when he was in the Scottish Office, you know. He wants to know whether you would meet him for lunch one day.'

'Where? In Sutherland?'

'No, in Edinburgh. It seems he's often in Edinburgh. I told him you'd let him know when you're off south again.'

'And what was the other message?'

'From the police in Dingwall. Two officers came round here in a car while you and Isobel were away and since then they have phoned twice. They seemed quite upset.'

'What did they want?'

'They didn't say, but they said you and Isobel should go to the station in Dingwall as soon as you got home.'

'It must be Isobel they want to talk to; about the fire.'

'Maybe, but the inspector was insistent that you should go to see them as well.'

*　　*　　*

'What I would like you to tell us,' Detective Inspector Dunlop said to Ian, 'is what your interest is in this business.'

Ian was not sure he understood the

question. 'My father was a close friend of Miss Gillespie's family.'

'I did not ask you what your interest in Miss Gillespie is, but why you are taking such an interest in the death of General Ballantine,' Dunlop said tersely and then without giving Ian time to reply, he continued, 'You see, Mr Blackie, we know that you were up at Ardnadaig recently asking questions about the General. I am assuming that was also why you went to see Miss Gillespie in her cottage.'

'Yes? And did you also know that not very long ago my father went to Ardnadaig to ask questions?' Learning that the police were aware of his movements and had perhaps been following him irritated Ian.

'We didn't, no.'

'My father believed that General Ballantine was not murdered by the IRA but he wished to find out who had killed him.'

'In that case why did he not come to the police?'

Inspector Dunlop seemed disconcerted and Ian realized that the initiative in the interview was now with him. When they had arrived at the police station, Isobel had been told that the police wished her to make a statement about the fire in her cottage. She had been taken to see the Chief Inspector and Ian had been kept waiting. Then several minutes later a constable had led him to an interview room where Dunlop and a sergeant had begun to question him.

'Perhaps he had no confidence in the police,' he replied, 'or it may have been that he had no reasons for his suspicions that he could give them.'

'So he went to Ardnadaig looking for evidence?'

'I believe so, yes.'

'Did he find any?'

'He must have found out that another man had been to Ardnadaig on the day General Ballantine died. We believe it was the same man that started the fire in Miss Gillespie's cottage. He had been to see her, claiming that he was the General's driver, but she knew the General did not have one.'

'What else do you know about this man?'

'Only that he was staying in a rented self-catering cottage not far from Ardnadaig at the time when the bomb was placed in the General's boat and he left there the day after the fire at Miss Gillespie's cottage.'

'Do you know his name?' Some of the irony in Dunlop's questions had softened. He was still sceptical, but Ian knew he had his attention.

'He gave the name of Frank Chalmers when he rented the cottage, but I imagine it was probably false.'

'Can you describe him?'

'I've never seen him,' Ian replied,

wondering whether the question had been a trick to catch him out in a lie. 'But Miss Gillespie has. This may help you.'

He took the sketch which he had made up at Shieldaig and handed it to Dunlop. Dunlop studied it carefully. 'Did you do this?'

'Yes. From the description Miss Gillespie gave me.'

'Very interesting. May I keep it?'

'By all means. Miss Gillespie believes that he may be a former soldier.'

'Oh, yes? Why is that?'

'Both her father and stepfather were soldiers. One might say that she was brought up in the Army.'

Dunlop did not immediately dismiss Isobel's reason as Ian thought he would. Instead, after a few moments' thought, he asked Ian, 'And your father? What were his reasons for thinking that General Ballantine was not murdered by the IRA?'

'He never told me, nor anyone else as far as I know.' Ian wondered whether he should tell Dunlop what he now believed, that Ballantine had gone to Ardnadaig to meet the IRA, but he decided not to. Opening up a conversation on that subject would cause too many complications, leading to too many awkward questions. His theory was in any case no more than speculative.

'So you went to Ardnadaig only because

your father had been there. Why?'

'I suppose you could say I was curious.'

'What did you do while you were there? To whom did you speak?'

'I'm sure you know that already, Inspector.' Ian was starting to be irritated once more.

'I know what other people have told me. Now I wish to hear your version.'

As patiently as he could Ian gave an account of his visit to Ardnadaig. Dunlop kept interrupting him, checking every point, tirelessly asking the same questions in different forms, making Ian repeat himself. The sergeant was making notes, but as far as Ian could tell the interview was not being recorded. Was that only done once a suspect had been charged with an offence? Ian was not sure. Finally it was over.

'You'll not leave your present address without informing us, will you?' Dunlop said. Ian explained that his home was in Edinburgh and he was uncertain of when he would be returning there. 'Then let us have both addresses and telephone numbers. The sergeant will take a note of them.'

When Ian returned to the entrance lobby he found that Isobel was not there. A constable on the desk told him that the young lady had just slipped out to the shops in Dingwall and would be back directly. Rather than wait for her inside the building,

Ian went out into the forecourt, which was a landscaped area with a small lawn and shrubs. Was it primordial feelings of guilt and fear, he wondered, that made him feel claustrophobic in police stations?

As he was standing in the forecourt a tall man in a tweed suit came out of the police station. As he passed Ian he glanced at him, but without interest or recognition. Ian knew at once that he had seen the man before, but it took him a few moments to remember that it had been at the Invermuir Golf Club dinner. Graeme Ross, the former Chief Constable of Tayside Police, had been one of the speakers that night.

CHAPTER NINE

The day was perfect for showing off Scotland's beauty; not one of those rare days of cloudless skies for which visitors hope, but one on which the haze of sunshine masks the contours of the mountains and the silent, brooding lochs. Instead moving clouds and fickle light gave those startling changes of colour on the hills, ranging from the palest of greens to indigo. As they approached the climb up to Drumochter pass they passed Dalwhinnie. The village where, Ian told Isobel, Queen Victoria had once spent a

night and complained of having to dine on
two starved Highland chickens, had been left
isolated by the construction of the new road
from Inverness to the south. Now it lay
forlorn, a ghost village made to seem even
more ghostly by the skeleton-white walls of
its distillery.

They talked of their visit to the police
station the previous day. 'They kept you a
long time,' Isobel remarked. 'I simply told
them about the fire and that was all.'

'I feel that they may suspect me of having
started the fire.'

'You can't be serious!'

'They must find it odd that I should have
turned up at your place on the afternoon
before the fire and the reason I gave may not
have sounded all that convincing.'

'Morons!' Isobel said angrily and then she
added, 'I'm glad you did turn up.' The
remark sounded neither coy nor flirtatious,
but unstudied, completely matter-of-fact.

'So am I, even though I may have been the
cause of the fire.'

'For God's sake! If you say that again, I'll
hit you.'

They had passed the loneliest stretch of
moors and were driving towards a
spectacular backcloth of mountains, the
peaks capped with snow. Isobel had told Ian
that she had never made that journey before
and he wished they had been driving down in

128

the late afternoon. At that time of the year, when the sun was beginning to set, the beauty of the mountains around Loch Ericht was almost unbelievable, the snow a delicate pink and the corries grey merging into browns.

It may have been the view that prompted Isobel to remark, 'You're pretty useful with a pencil, aren't you, Ian?'

'Sketching has always been a hobby of mine.'

'In my bedroom at your parents' home there was a watercolour on one wall; a Highland scene. Was that your work?'

'It is, although I don't boast about it. I did that when I was fourteen as I remember. My grandparents could not be dissuaded from having it framed. You know how grandparents are.'

'Where did you paint it? In Wester Ross?'

'No, on Skye. Turner and a few thousand Victorian ladies have done better.'

'Do you still paint?'

'Hardly ever. There's never enough time.'

'Would you do a watercolour for me? I'd love to have one in my cottage when I return to it.'

Her question caught Ian mentally off-balance. Isobel was looking at him as she asked it, as though to show it was not just a meaningless politeness. What made him cautious was a feeling that by asking the question she was opening the way for their relationship to change and become closer. She may not have meant that nor even been aware of it, but he hesitated before he answered. He had not even begun to consider whether he wished theirs to be anything more than a casual friendship.

'I will if I can find the time.'

Isobel had noticed the hesitation. She said, 'That was cheeky of me, was it not?'

Immediately Ian felt ashamed. He had read too much into the question no doubt and after what she had endured over the past two days, Isobel deserved a less churlish response. 'Not at all. I'm flattered. I'll tell you what I'll do. When you're back in the cottage I'll come up and paint that wonderful view over Loch Torridon to the mountains of Kintail.'

'Why not out over the Inner Sound to the Cuillins of Skye?'

'That as well, if you like. Then you'll have two.'

'Brilliant!'

By the time they were drawing near Pitlochry, Ian felt that Isobel might be growing weary of the journey, and as they moved further south driving along the motorway would become monotonous. So he left the A9 and drove into Pitlochry to stop for a coffee. They walked through the town and as they were passing a shop selling woollens and tweeds Isobel saw a pink lambswool sweater in the window which she decided to buy. In Dingwall the previous day she had bought a pair of burgundy-coloured slacks and the sweater would be perfect with them. Ever since the fire she had been wearing slacks, he noticed, never once putting on the skirt his mother had brought home for her from the charity shop.

When they were leaving Pitlochry he suggested that they take the old scenic road to Dunkeld and Perth which wound its way through woodland. Not far short of Dunkeld they passed a mini-bus which had stopped by the side of the road and was disgorging its passengers. They were all men, dressed for climbing, and some were carrying ropes. A sign painted on the side of the mini-bus advertised 'Endurance Holidays' and gave an address and telephone number in Dundee.

One of the men leaving the mini-bus seemed vaguely familiar. Ian said to Isobel, 'That man we just passed looked rather like the mysterious Frank Chalmers.'

Isobel turned round to look behind her. 'Where?'

'Too late now. He had the same eyebrows.'

'What you mean is that he looked like your sketch of the man. Your identikit picture could fit every villain in Scotland.'

'You're probably right.'

131

Ian supposed that he should not be surprised at seeing the bus, for outdoor holidays in Scotland were most likely to be taken in the Highlands and they were not far from Dundee where the holiday company was based. One could not even think of it as a coincidence, but it was even so a reminder of his father's involvement with General Ballantine and whatever secret group the two of them had formed or joined.

Another, although more oblique, reminder came when they reached Edinburgh and he had stopped the car outside his flat in Dean village. He had forgotten that it was in Dean Cemetery that Sir Hector Macdonald, the hero of Omdurman who had risen from the ranks to be a general, had been buried almost secretly and in shame. Ian recalled how Bruce Niven had drawn an analogy between what had happened to Sir Hector and General Ballantine's treatment by Edinburgh society.

He had bought the flat in the village just over a year previously and was still rather proud of it. The new development of which it was a part had been widely praised in the architectural press for the way it had been designed to merge into its surroundings and retain the charm of the village. Other new buildings had been attacked as totally out of keeping with what was essentially a rural area. When he showed Isobel round the flat, he was disappointed that she did not seem to be impressed. Leaving her in the bedroom she was to use to put away the few belongings she had brought in an airline bag, he went to his own bedroom to unpack. His mother had insisted that he should stay in Edinburgh for at least two days and she had invited her sister to join her in Invermuir while he was away.

'Just you make sure the poor girl is properly settled in before you leave,' she had told Ian.

Isobel's first priority was to go shopping, she said, and when she was ready he walked with her up to Queensferry Street where she would be able to hail a taxi. She refused his offer of a loan of money for her shopping and it was only after persuasion that she accepted ten pounds to pay for the taxi.

'I'm beginning to feel like a kept woman,' she said as she took the note.

'That's absurd!'

'Don't worry. I rather enjoy the feeling!'

Back in the flat he switched on his word processor and inserted the disc which Isobel had given him up at Shieldaig. Finding the copies she had made of Ballantine's papers did not take long for she had put them on to an almost unused disc. Presently the first page came up on the screen. It was headed TRAINING SCHEDULE and at first glance appeared to consist only of a series of numbers and letters. Ian studied it.

TRAINING SCHEDULE

Week 1

Sq A	82	174	203	232
Sq B	30	71	120	228
Sq C	26	75	76	123
Sq D	49	96	133	162
Sq E	53	58	95	260
Sq F	AC			

Week 2

Sq A	26	75	76	123
Sq B	49	96	133	162
Sq C	53	78	95	260
Sq D	82	174	203	252
Sq E	30	71	120	128
Sq F	WT			

Week 3	Week 4
AC	WT
WT	AC
AC	WT
WT	AC
AC	WT
RC	RC

If this were a training schedule for a sports club, for boxers or athletes say, Ian supposed that the Sq might stand for squads. Squad training was very much the fashion in all forms of sport now. He remembered too that Ballantine had been President of the Soldiers Resettlement Association, which might well organize sporting activities for its members. He was also a director of a firm making sports equipment.

Ian had no idea what either the letters or the numbers might mean. They could be some form of code, he supposed, but what possible reason could there be for writing a sports training programme in code? What could Ballantine have been trying to conceal? Ian noticed that Squad F had a different programme to the other squads. Could this mean that it was an élite squad being trained for a special purpose?

The second page was even more cryptic than the first. Isobel had typed a note on the top of it which read, 'NB. This sheet and the remaining ones were both handwritten on what looked like pages torn from a memo pad. I am reasonably sure the handwriting was Sandy's.' Below her note were what looked like mathematical formulae and beneath them words jotted apparently at random.

$$60 \times AK47 \times 280 = 16800$$
$$BT \quad \underline{10000}$$
$$6800$$

D 52 477401–477440
B 33 816081–816120
C 28 606141–606180
D 48 522833–522848

NOTES

Javelins
Lightweight M.Ls ?
Big bang–1012
loco–Queen St station?

Confirm R-V DMO
Tues. Sprinter 0930

Ian supposed there might be some connection with the notes and the training schedule. Javelins might be required for an athletic club, whose members would no doubt include sprinters, and lightweights could be boxers. He also wondered whether the letters R-V might refer to a rendezvous with the DMO which Ballantine must remember to confirm.

On the third page there were only a few lines, evidently written with difficulty for a number of words had been scratched out. If they had been composed by Ballantine, as Isobel believed, then his spelling had not improved since he left school.

PROCLAMATION

We, as representatives of the XXXXXXXXXX soverein State of Scotland make the following demands to the British Government:

1. that it gives an irrevocable committment forthwith to grant Scotland full independence,
2. that a XXXXXXXXXX constitution for Scotland be

A picture came to Ian's mind of Ballantine working on his proclamation in Isobel's cottage on the evening before he drove down to Ardnadaig for his meeting with the IRA. He wondered what might have happened to prevent him from finishing it.

He passed on to the final page of the papers. This also carried a list of numbers and letters and it was headed SCOTLAND ARISE–EMERGENCY CODES. The list beneath the heading read:

PM	652338040
CE	692127990
HO	101838370
FO	05230260
MH	44847430
MI	182322830
AG	7104455130
DMO	5441149140

By the time he had studied all the papers for a second time, Ian was surrendering to disbelief. That grown men, some of them past retirement age, should go to such lengths to conceal whatever they were plotting, seemed childish as well as paranoid. The papers Ballantine had left in Isobel's cottage confirmed that Ballantine and his father had been involved in a Scottish nationalist organization of some kind and he guessed that they had given it the name Scotland Arise. Not a bad name for a group if it was to be militant, he was prepared to admit. But the papers told him nothing of what Scotland Arise planned to do nor, more importantly for Ian, what role his father had played in it and why Sandy Ballantine had been murdered.

Once again he was beginning to feel that he had stumbled on to an adolescent fantasy which would never take practical shape and that he should not waste time trying to decipher its puzzles. Reluctantly he printed out two copies of everything that was on Isobel's disc and switched off the word processor. Even more reluctantly he decided as a precaution to leave only one copy in the flat and to take the other with him. You're growing paranoid too, he told himself.

He walked round to his company's offices

in Melville Street and spent an hour there, fifteen minutes talking with one of his two partners and the remainder with Rosemary deciding how to deal with the few letters that were waiting for his attention. On the way back to Dean village he stopped at a newsagent to pick up a copy of the *Evening Times* and while he was there bought that day's *Scotsman* as well. In Invermuir it was easy to lose touch with the national and international news and for the last few days he had not picked up a newspaper nor watched television.

The front-page story in both papers was the minor storm that had arisen over the visit to Scotland by the Queen which was to take place later that week. The United Kingdom was to be the host of a meeting of the heads of member states in the enlarged European Community and it had been decided that this should be held in Edinburgh. The Queen would be entertaining the heads of state in her Palace of Holyroodhouse and the *pièce de résistance* of the three-day visit was to be a dinner in the Great Hall of Edinburgh Castle.

Holding the meeting in Edinburgh had been intended as a compliment to Scotland, but the compliment had turned sour over a tiny matter of flags. A story had been 'leaked' that the Royal Mile, up which the Queen and her guests would drive to the Castle, was to be decorated with clusters of flags, the flags of the Community Member States alternating with Union Jacks. Nowhere was Scotland's own flag, the St Andrew's Cross, to be flown. Coming soon after the news that the European Commissioner for Energy had floated a proposal for taking over Scotland's off-shore oil reserves and paying Great Britain—not Scotland—compensation, the supposed insult of the flags had been blown up into a bitter row. Even though the organizers of the meeting had now climbed down over the matter of the flags, the anger and the bitterness had not subsided and still dominated the news.

Just at the back of seven o'clock Isobel returned to the flat. Ian watched her leaving the taxi and noticed that she was carrying only a small brown paper bag. She came into the flat looking happy and offered her cheek to be kissed.

'Don't tell me you couldn't find anything to buy,' he said.

'You're joking! I've been on a gargantuan shopping spree. Knowing that the insurance company would be paying I lost all self-restraint. Everything is being delivered here tomorrow. I hope you don't mind.' She held up the paper bag. 'All I brought home was this. You won't believe it but I went into James Thin and bought one of my own books.'

140

'What's wrong with that?'

'Nothing I suppose, but I felt self-conscious as I pulled it out of the shelves. I don't know why I did it; just to prove to myself that I am an author perhaps.'

'May I see it?'

The book had a board cover decorated with a simple pattern of orange flowers and green leaves. The title suggested that it told the story of two golden eagle chicks growing up, one a clever swot, the other obsessed with sport. As Ian glanced through the pages, Isobel dropped into an armchair.

'Did you print out that disc?' she asked.

'I did, and as you said all I found was a cryptic mass of numbers. They mean nothing to me.'

'I'll take a look at them. It's strange. People say one is either literate or numerate and I suppose I'm literate, but I seem to have an instinct for numbers.'

'Was there nothing else in Sandy Ballantine's briefcase?'

'Only two maps; street maps of Inverness and Fort William.'

'I would not have thought that Fort William is large enough to have a street map.'

'You're probably right. What Sandy had was cut out of the very large-scale Ordnance Survey map.'

'I suppose he needed them for his drive up

to your place.'

'That's not likely. He drove up the A9, which rules out Fort William, and when he arrived he remarked how much quicker the drive is now one can cross the Moray Firth by the new bridge and bypass Inverness completely.'

'In that case why would he have brought the maps?'

Isobel shrugged her shoulders. 'Let's take a look at the stuff on the disc tomorrow, shall we?'

'Sure. There's no great urgency.'

'Meantime shall I cook us a meal?'

'No way! We'll dine out. There's no food in the flat anyway.'

'Would you mind if I don't change? I'm knackered after all that shopping.'

'Of course I won't. You've nothing to change into anyway, have you?'

'No, not until tomorrow.'

They agreed to eat in the Kwelin, a Chinese restaurant in Dundas Street. As they walked there, Isobel told Ian of the new book on which she was working. The principal character in the story was a young pine marten, an animal once almost extinct, but now to be found again in Scotland. Ian had heard that they were to be found in the forests around Beinn Eighe. The pine marten in Isobel's story was, without knowing it, a mathematical genius, able to

142

make phenomenal and unbelievably rapid calculations. Isobel explained to Ian that she always tried to have an educational element, suitably disguised, in her stories.

As they were walking along Heriot Row, she took his hand in hers, so easily and naturally that at first he did not notice what she had done. Once again he began to ask himself whether they were slipping into a kind of intimacy and whether he should welcome it. He hoped his uneasiness did not show. Not until they were in the restaurant and had ordered their meal did he decide that she had instinctively guessed what he might be thinking.

'Has your mother ever stayed with you in your flat?'

'No. Why do you ask?'

'I thought I detected traces of, how shall I put it, a feminine presence in the bathroom.'

'Until a few weeks ago a girlfriend was living with me.'

'Do you want to tell me about it?'

Ian remembered then that he had asked Isobel exactly the same question when she had told him of the holiday she had spent in a Highland shieling with a boy. He resisted the temptation to make the same reply as she had then. Instead he said, 'Why not?'

He told her about Jennifer, who had lived with him for more than a year in a flat which they had rented jointly in Morningside.

When he bought the property in Dean village Jennifer had moved with him, but almost immediately their relationship had begun to change. Jennifer had seemed almost to resent his owning the flat and would make snide remarks about capitalism and bourgeois respectability, which were scarcely in character, for she had been brought up as a Tory and never previously shown any inclination to socialist or even liberal views. After a few uncomfortable and fractious months, she had moved out and back to Morningside.

'Maybe she didn't like my new flat, couldn't bear living there.'

'Then she must be very hard to please.'

'You didn't seem very impressed when I showed you round today.' Ian hoped his remark did not sound peevish.

'That isn't true. It's very attractive and you've decorated it with real taste!' Isobel said, and for some reason Ian had the feeling she was embarrassed. Then she added, 'To be honest I was thinking how shabby my cottage must have seemed to you in comparison.'

Intuition told Ian not to pursue the matter. He would have liked to tell her about the sheets of numbers in the papers Sandy Ballantine had left with her, but he sensed that the traumatic effects of having her cottage burnt down were beginning to fade and he had no wish to revive them. So instead they talked of life in Edinburgh, his work and his friends.

Presently Ian said, 'We might have dinner with a friend of mine and his wife tomorrow evening, if you like.'

The friend he had in mind was Bruce Niven, for he had questions he would like to ask Bruce, and he was surprised when Isobel did not reply. Then he saw that her eyes were closed. She had dozed off at the table, a thing he had sometimes done himself, but only when he had been exhausted by overwork. He shook her arm gently.

'Come on. I'm taking you home.'

Too tired even to protest, she allowed him to pay the bill, order a taxi, and leave the restaurant, even though neither of them had finished their meal. On the short ride home, her head slid on to his shoulder as she slept again. When they reached the flat, he went with her to the door of her bedroom.

'Is there anything you need?'

She kissed him on the cheek. 'Only sleep.'

Alone in the sitting-room of the flat, Ian felt restless and wondered what to do. On a normal day he would usually bring work home from the office and he had got out of the habit of watching television except for the nightly news programme. He had no wish to entangle himself in trying to make sense out of Ballantine's papers, so he

145

decided to read Isobel's book, which she had left lying on a table.

After reading only a few pages he was aware of the skill and sensitivity in her writing. The story, the characters, and their sentiments were all childlike, but the dialogue resembled a child's attempt at 'grown-up' conversation. By flattering a child's aspirations, she would in a subtle way be drawing out its intelligence.

Putting the book down, he found a sheet of paper and to amuse himself began sketching. He drew the figures of two golden eagle chicks, one wearing spectacles and reading a massive book, the other playing golf.

Before he had finished the sketch the telephone interrupted him and he was surprised to hear Tristram Stewart's voice. 'Is that you, Ian? I heard that you were back in Edinburgh.'

'Only briefly. I shall need to return to Invermuir in a day or so.'

'Then I'm glad I caught you. Would you be free to lunch with me tomorrow? I have a proposition to put to you.'

The way the invitation was phrased did not allow for a refusal and Ian recognized the arrogance of a successful politician. In any case there was no reason why he should refuse.

'Shall we make it the New Club, then? At

twelve-thirty?'

After he had put the phone down, Ian began to wonder what proposition Stewart had in mind to make. He supposed it would be a follow-up to his conversation with Donald Buchanan at Loch Maree distillery. By now the current financial year's accounts of the West Highland Scotch Whisky Company might be available and the company might have funds to invest. Stewart was chairman of the Tayside Rope Company, which had interlocking directorships with the whisky company and might well be advising it.

The phone call reminded him that he had intended to ring his mother that evening. She liked him to call her when he arrived in Edinburgh after driving down from Invermuir, just to reassure her that he had made the journey safely. He also wished to reassure himself that her sister had arrived to keep her company and that both of them were all right.

She was all right and in good voice, delighted to hear from him and determined to bring him up to date with the unspectacular family news that her sister had brought. Just as she was about to ring off, he told her of the call from Tristram Stewart.

'We're lunching together tomorrow. I suppose you must have told him that I would be in Edinburgh.'

147

'Ian, you're getting very forgetful,' Mrs Blackie said reproachfully. 'As bad as Monica MacBain. I told you yesterday that he had rung up to speak to you.'

'Then he didn't phone you today?'

'No. Why should he have?'

After he had put the phone down, Ian wondered how Stewart could possibly have known that he was in Edinburgh. He had only told his mother late the previous evening that he would be driving down with Isobel today. He fought down a temptation to do what characters did in old Hollywood films, and did not peer through a chink in the curtains to see whether there might be a shadowy figure watching in the lane outside the flat.

CHAPTER TEN

Next morning soon after breakfast Isobel left the flat, on foot this time. She was heading for the West End branch of the Royal Bank of Scotland, where she had arranged to see the manager, so that her account, which was still in the Selkirk branch, could be transferred to Edinburgh. From there she intended to go to the Central Library on George IV Bridge, for she needed to find out more about the habits of pine martens.

'Then, if you won't be using your WPC,' she had said, 'I'll come back and start writing. I'll need to be here this afternoon, for the shops will be delivering all the goodies I bought yesterday.'

After she had gone, Ian pulled out the copies of Ballantine's papers which he had run off on the word processor's printer the previous evening. He would not look in at his office again, for he did not wish to become involved in any of the work that was currently being done there. It would be unfair to start interfering with any projects which his colleagues might have begun until his holiday was over. His present intention was to return to Invermuir in a couple of days or as soon as Isobel had organized herself in the flat. His mother's sister could not stay with her indefinitely.

Before he began studying Ballantine's papers, he remembered that he should ring Bruce Niven, who would probably not yet have left home for the offices of the *Scotsman*. Forgetting that he was not in Invermuir, he punched out the Edinburgh prefix 031 before Bruce's number and then, realizing his mistake, began again. Bruce was still at home and he and his wife gladly accepted Ian's invitation to have dinner with himself and Isobel.

'What's Isobel Gillespie doing in Edinburgh?' Bruce asked. 'I was under the

149

impression that she was more or less a recluse in Wester Ross.'

'It's a long story. We'll tell you this evening.'

As he was finishing the call, Ian glanced at the copy of Ballantine's papers which lay on the table by the telephone. On top was the single sheet of numbers, originally handwritten as Isobel had noted. One of the numbers, he noticed, ended with the three digits 130, which was the reverse of the Edinburgh code which he had just dialled by mistake. There were ten digits in the number altogether—7104455130. Could it simply be a telephone number written in reverse? The idea seemed far-fetched, but there was a simple way of finding out whether it was and whether it was the number of one of Ballantine's little circle. He punched the number out on the phone and heard a ringing tone.

Several seconds passed and then he heard a woman's voice. 'Jennifer Roxburgh here.'

Ian apologized for having called a wrong number, put down the phone, and then looked at the list of numbers in astonishment. Could Ballantine's secret code be no more than a list of telephone numbers that he might have to use in an emergency and which he had tried to disguise simply by reversing them? Ian remembered the message which Ballantine had sent to his father on the microcassette and in which he had spoken of 'telephone silence'. In wartime pilots of aircraft had sometimes to maintain radio silence. He remembered too that Ballantine had been afraid that his own telephone was being tapped. To test his theory he found the Edinburgh telephone directory and found an entry for David Roxburgh QC, who had an address in Crammond and his phone number was the one which Ian had just called.

He looked at the list again and saw that one of the numbers ended in the digits 7430, which when reversed was the telephone code number for Invermuir. The remaining digits were also familiar and he realized that the whole number when reversed was a phone number he knew well, for it belonged to Dr Nicholas MacBain.

The number at the bottom of the list, which was separated slightly from the others, ended with the digits 140. When reversed that was the telephone code for Glasgow. He punched out the full number and this time a man's voice answered, sharply and rudely, with just the one word 'Hullo'.

Putting the phone down, he studied the list more carefully. The amount of digits in each number varied from seven to ten, but the telephone codes used in Scotland, he knew, also varied. The codes for Edinburgh and Glasgow had only three digits, but some rural areas, he knew, had six-figure codes. Telephone numbers themselves also varied in length from three digits to seven. One way of checking whether these were phone numbers and to whom they belonged would be to ring each of the numbers. He rejected the idea, because whoever answered each call might not give his name. One could also not discount the possibility that one of the people answering might recognize his voice.

Finding out to whom each of the numbers belonged should not present an insurmountable problem, but in the meantime he was puzzled by the letters which preceded each number. At first he had thought they might be the initials of the owners of the numbers, but the letters before David Roxburgh's number were AG and those before Nick MacBain's were MH. The letters against the number at the bottom of the list were DMO. They sounded vaguely familiar and he remembered then that in his recorded message to Ian's father, Sandy Ballantine had made a reference to 'the DMO'.

He copied the numbers and letters on to the back of an old envelope which was lying on the table and put the envelope in his pocket. Then he left the flat, like Isobel on foot, and set out for the General Post Office in Waterloo Place.

Knowing that he needed exercise, he did

not follow the direct route but, on reaching Princes Street, dropped down into the gardens below the castle. There, after passing the open-air theatre, he crossed the railway and climbed up the bank on the far side, until he reached Mound Place and then cut into Castlehill. As he walked down the Royal Mile he saw workmen erecting the poles from which the flags would be erected for the Queen's visit, assuming that the argument over the issue was ever resolved. On the corner of North Bridge a kilted piper, a slim young man immaculate in his Gordon tartan, was playing, with an upturned Glengarry bonnet on the pavement in front of him. One could often find pipers in the streets of Edinburgh and not only in Edinburgh. Ian had seen them in the Trossachs, playing at strategic points where they knew that tourists in cars or buses would stop to admire a particularly fine view. Seeing them would provoke a spurt of anger in him. Was this all that was left of the heritage of Scotland, the great legends, the heroism in battles all over the world, the poignant laments for dead heroes? A piper playing for the pennies of pitying foreigners? And if independence came, was this what it would mean for Scotland? Surviving on the hand-outs of her English neighbours or of the European Community?

At the post office his anger turned to

irritation when he learned that telephone directories were no longer kept there. Once there had been a set of all the directories covering Scotland, but so many were stolen or defaced that the practice had been abandoned. Ian was told that he would find a set in the Central Public Library on George IV Bridge. As he made his way there, he remembered that Isobel had gone to the same library to do her research into pine martens. If he did see her, he hoped she would not think that he had followed her there.

When he was shown the set of directories, he pulled out the envelope on which he had copied Sandy Ballantine's list of numbers. He was confident that he knew the names of the people to whom the numbers might belong, so checking that his theory was correct was not difficult, although working his way through several directories took time. Eventually he was able to make his own list of the names and numbers. Although he could not see what significance the letters against each of the numbers could have, he added them as well.

Golspie 3256	Tristram Stewart	PM
Strathpeffer 21296	Donald Buchanan	CE
Perth 38101	Graeme Ross	HO
North Berwick 3250	Douglass Wreford	FO
Invermuir 4844	Nick MacBain	MH

Dundee 23281	Peter Walters	MI
Edinburgh 554–4017	David Roxburgh	AG
Glasgow 941–1445	?	DMO

The names on the list he had compiled, Ian assumed, must represent all the members or at least the core of Ballantine's secret organization, Scotland Arise. They were the people whom Ballantine might have needed to contact in an emergency if anything had gone wrong with the arrangements he had made for his rendezvous with Sean Deeney and telephone silence had to be broken. Andrew Blackie's phone number was not on the list, but that would be because Ballantine must have known it well.

There was nothing surprising in the fact that his father and Ballantine had formed a Scottish nationalist group, for new such groups of one type or another were being formed almost every week. What still puzzled Ian was the close and almost comical secrecy with which the group's plans and membership had been cloaked. He looked at the letters against each name and particularly at the one at the top of the list. 'PM' was a much-used abbreviation, especially by civil servants. His father had never referred to the Prime Minister in any other way.

Realization came like a sudden burst of gunfire, each truth exploding in rapid

155

succession. Ballantine's group had done what more than one other organization working for Scottish independence had done, drawn up plans for a provisional government to run Scotland once independence was granted or was won. Tristram Stewart was to be the Prime Minister and, as Ian looked at the list, the other cabinet offices fell into place. Donald Buchanan had been selected as Chancellor of the Exchequer, although Ian wondered what qualifications he had for the post, and Graeme Ross, a former Chief Constable, would be minister in charge of the Home Office. The remaining selections seemed appropriate enough if Ian's interpretation of the letters were correct. Peter Walters was to be Minister for Industry, Wreford the head of the Foreign Office and MacBain Minister for Health.

The letters against Roxburgh's name, he supposed, might designate Attorney-General or perhaps Advocate-General, as the Parliament was to be Scottish. That left only Ballantine and his father. Ballantine would surely have been earmarked as Minister for Defence and his father, shunning the limelight of a portfolio, would probably have been content with, say, Leader of the House of Parliament or Secretary to the Cabinet.

As he was leaving the library he did see Isobel. She was coming up the stairs from one of the specialized libraries in the lower floors of the building, talking earnestly to a man of about Ian's age. Ian's first impulse was to wait for her to reach him, but he decided not to, knowing that he was in danger of being late for his appointment with Tristram Stewart.

Once again, as he walked down the Mound towards the New Club, he had the feeling that he had accidentally strayed into a world of fantasy. He could understand that a group of patriotic Scots might unite to work for Scottish self-rule, if not total independence. Others had done it before and he had every sympathy for their aspirations, but the secrecy with which Ballantine had surrounded what Scotland Arise was planning and his negotiations with the IRA seemed unreal, not so much sinister as farcical. And yet one of Scotland's best-known generals was dead and the cottage of an innocent author had been destroyed. He found himself wondering uneasily what kind of adventures the two ageing adolescents, Ballantine and his father, might have dreamt up.

To him the New Club was itself not far divorced from fantasy. A weird anachronism, its new building of ugly concrete slabs sheltered relics of a distant and leisurely age, fine furniture and paintings of statesmen. On the walls in the library and the passages, the club rooms and the bedrooms hung a bizarre variety of old prints, scenes of old Edinburgh, portraits of Burns and Scott and of dukes and their huntsmen. And most incongruous touch of all, the club's entrance in Princes Street was alongside a shop selling cots and babies' clothes. Ian could not imagine that the club's members, moving above its ceiling painfully on arthritic limbs, would ever bring the shop much business.

Tristram Stewart was waiting for him in the Members' bar. Watching him as he ordered two whiskies for them, Ian thought that the man might well make a good Prime Minister for Scotland. He had the bearing and manner of a Scottish aristocrat, but was a good deal more intelligent than any of the aristocrats who Ian knew. He was also, in Ian's view, more intelligent and shrewder than the Scot then occupying 10 Downing Street, which may well have been the reason why his political career had been abruptly cut short.

When he returned with the whiskies, he said to Ian, 'I've asked David Roxburgh to join us for lunch. Do you know him?'

'I know of him of course, but we have never met.'

'You'll not mind his lunching with us?'

'Not at all. Why should I?'

'Some people might be suspicious that I'm bringing a lawyer with me.' Stewart smiled.

158

'But as you'll find out it's all quite innocent.'

They chatted for a while, with Stewart reminiscing about his days at the Scottish Office and mentioning some of the occasions when Ian's father had worked with him. The compliments he paid Andrew Blackie were in no way fulsome, but praised his dedication and loyalty. Ian knew the compliments must have been deserved, for he had often heard others speak in the same vein. Stewart also told him that his father's abilities had been recognized in the service as well and that he had been offered the decoration given to many senior civil servants on their retirement, but his father had refused it. Ian had not known that, but he was not surprised.

Soon David Roxburgh arrived to join them. He was a short, powerfully built man, already portly, although he would not be much past forty, and with a massive head that reminded one of the plaster busts of Beethoven once to be seen on the mantelpieces of houses in Craigmillar. The three of them took their whiskies into the morning room, which was adjacent to the bar and where, Stewart said, they would be able to talk more freely. Their conversation at first, though, was in no way private.

'They've made a real cock-up of this EC meeting and the Queen's visit, have they not?' Roxburgh said.

'Holding it in Scotland is meant as a sop to us Scots, to take our minds off independence,' Stewart replied. 'God only knows who was responsible for the blunder with the flags, but it's typical of the way in which Whitehall treats us.'

'The geriatric old soldiers will be happy for a chance to parade in the Lincoln green. I see they were down shooting for their silver arrow on Leith Links last week.' Roxburgh turned to Ian. 'I trust you have no aspirations to be a member of the Royal Company of Archers, Ian.'

Ian laughed. 'Not quite my scene, I think, even if I were to live long enough to qualify.'

'What do you feel about devolution?' Stewart asked him.

'In my opinion we Scots have the right to govern ourselves.'

'Your father would have agreed with you,' Stewart said. 'He served Scotland as well as anyone, but he would never take any medals handed out in Whitehall.'

'I'm not sure about independence though,' Ian said. 'Do you think this is the right time for it?'

'Why not? Independence is in the air. The Croats, the Basques, the Lithuanians, they all want it and they will all get it. The Russian Empire has disintegrated and so will England's precious Union.'

The argument, if it could be called one,

160

was still unresolved when they went into the dining-room. Not until they had finished lunch and were having coffee and a whisky in the library did Stewart raise the matter he wished to discuss with Ian, and then he raised it only obliquely.

'For a club of its standing the selection of malt whiskies in the New Club is disgracefully small.'

'Why don't you raise the matter with the directors?' Roxburgh asked.

'I believe I will.' Stewart turned to Ian. 'You were up at Loch Maree distillery the other day, I understand.'

'Yes, Donald Buchanan invited me there.'

'Donald's a good lad.' A flicker of ill-humour soured Stewart's expression, but only briefly. 'I've never cared much for his father, but Donald's all right.'

'He is,' Roxburgh agreed. 'He's made good, has Donald, in spite of his father. There's never been much love between them.'

'What did you think of the distillery?'

'I was impressed. And the company's accounts appear very sound.'

'You've seen the accounts?' Stewart asked; rather quickly it seemed to Ian.

'Yes. When Donald Buchanan said he might wish to consult my company on investments, I made a point of obtaining a copy of the West Highland Scotch Whisky

Company's last annual report and accounts.'

'Very sensible!' Stewart looked at Roxburgh and smiled. 'I told you, David, that the lad is shrewd as well as clever.'

'Then you'll know that your father was a director of the company?'

'Yes, although he never told me so himself.'

'Does that surprise you?'

'Not really. In many ways my dad was rather a private man.'

'And you'll know that David is on the board of the company and that I once was. The reason we invited you to meet us here today, Ian, is that the directors would like you to replace your father.'

Ian stared at him incredulously. 'To join the board?'

'Precisely.'

'But why me? Because of my father?'

'I'll not deny that there may be a touch of sentiment in our choice of you,' Stewart said smiling, 'but as you well know, no true Scot allows sentiment to overcome his best interests. No, Ian lad, it's your particular talents that the company is after.'

He explained that the West Highland Scotch Whisky Company had now lost two of its directors, General Ballantine and Andrew Blackie. On top of that no member of the board had any experience of finance or accountancy.

162

'General Wreford has been acting as chairman since poor Sandy's death,' Stewart said, 'and he will be the next chairman. Douggie had intended to be here to meet you today, but he stays at North Berwick and was prevented from coming in at the last minute.'

'Another reason why we are looking for another director,' Roxburgh told Ian, 'is that we've been one short since Tristram stepped down.'

'May I ask why you left the board, sir?'

'I may be returning to politics.' Stewart must have guessed what Ian was thinking, for he went on: 'Yes, I know that at your golf club dinner I said I had no wish to re-enter the political rat-race, but a lot of my friends have persuaded me otherwise. They have convinced me that I should put Scotland and Scotland's future before my personal inclinations.'

'Scotland's future! Does that mean you may be standing as a Scottish Nationalist?'

Stewart looked around him furtively, as though to see whether anyone were near enough to overhear what he was going to say. 'If they offer me the right seat I might. Independence is on the way, Ian lad. I'm convinced of that.'

'But it won't come before the next general election. And that could be not for another three years.'

163

'Maybe. On the other hand it could come much more quickly. This government is in trouble. But whenever it comes, I want to be ready and so I'm giving up all my directorships and other commitments.'

'Well, what do you think of our offer?' Roxburgh appeared to be growing impatient with the talk of politics. 'Does it appeal to you?'

'I'm very flattered to be asked of course, but I do have my work here in Edinburgh.'

'That need not be an impediment. Our board meetings are always held at Loch Maree distillery and you'll be needing to go up to Invermuir more often, I imagine, now that your mother is alone, so...' Stewart did not need to finish his sentence.

'May I think about it?'

'By all means. There's no great urgency. I shall be away from Edinburgh for the next few days, until all the flag-waving is over. I couldn't bear the sight of Scots being servile to foreigners.'

'To the EC heads of state?'

'I was thinking of the English,' Stewart smiled. 'Let me know your decision after the royal visit is over.'

As he walked along Princes Street in the direction of Dean village, Ian decided that the offer of a directorship in the whisky company could not be just coincidence. Stewart and the other members of Sandy

Ballantine's group must know of the interest he had been taking in Sandy's death. They would too know of the fire at Isobel's cottage and of his interview by the police at Dingwall. That Graeme Ross, a member of Sandy's group and a former policeman, should have been at the police station that afternoon might have been an accident of chance. Ian thought not. If, as he suspected, he had been followed down to Edinburgh, they would also know that Isobel was with him.

The lunch at the New Club could well have been a subtle ploy. Stewart's frankness could have been intended to convince Ian that he and his friends were no more than just another nationalist group, working passionately but harmlessly for Scottish independence. If he was not convinced of their harmlessness, the directorship could be a bribe to make sure that he would align himself with them.

CHAPTER ELEVEN

From the New Club Ian walked round to his firm's offices in Melville Street. The offer of a directorship had made him curious to know more about the West Highland Scotch Whisky Company. Rosemary, his secretary, was not busy, so he asked her to help in his search for information. He telephoned Jock Waugh, an analyst who worked for a Glasgow firm of stockbrokers and who was said to know more than anyone about the Scotch whisky business.

What Jock had to say was interesting. The early 1980s had seen a slump in the whisky trade. Because of excessive production over a number of years, the stocks of whisky in Scotland were far too large and production was then cut back severely, to not much more than half of what it had been. Many distilleries had stopped distilling altogether. Some had been closed, never to reopen, while others had been 'put in mothballs' until the slump ended. Neither of the West Highland Scotch Whisky Company's distilleries, Loch Maree and Glen Torridon, had been closed, and both had continued distilling. This had been an act of benevolence on the part of the owners, who had not wished to see the distillery workers lose their jobs. Production had been cut, but even so a substantial stock of maturing whisky had been built up which most people in the trade thought would never be sold.

In the last year or two however, Jock had told Ian, the company's trading position had shown a remarkable improvement. The Buchanan family, which had financed the distillery out of their own money during the slump, had handed over control to a consortium. Alisdair Buchanan had pulled out of the business altogether as soon as he had become Prime Minister and a new board of directors was running the company.

'The new board seem to have put the company on its feet,' Jock had concluded, 'although no one quite knows how. The management are very secretive. My guess is that they have done a deal with the Japanese and are shipping their stocks of malt whisky in casks to Japan, where it is being used to improve the quality of Japanese whisky.'

'Is that allowed?'

'Oh yes. Bloody foolish, if you want my opinion, but perfectly legitimate.'

Jock had added that if Ian wished to know more about the trade in malt whisky with Japan he should get hold of a copy of *The Spirit of Whisky*, a paperback book which had recently been published. It made fascinating reading, he said.

While Ian had been on the phone, Rosemary had finished her own research, also by telephone. He had been curious to know how it was that the appointment of General Wreford as chairman of the West Highland Scotch Whisky Company should have been reported in the *Financial Times*. The company was very small, owned privately and therefore not quoted on the stock exchange. Space in the FT's appointments columns was limited and much in demand for announcing the career movements of high-fliers in industry and commerce. The paper must have had some special reason for publishing Wreford's appointment, Ian thought.

'Apparently the FT got it from a press release issued by the company's consultants,' Rosemary told him.

'Who are the consultants?'

'A London firm named Westminster Confidential. It's run by Montgomerie Banks, an old Fleet Street type, and it seems to carry a lot of clout.'

'Sounds rather grand as PR consultants for an obscure whisky company.'

'I agree. Especially as they are not in PR but are parliamentary consultants. They do a lot of work for foreign governments, arranging for groups of British MPs to visit countries which are trying to have friends in Westminster; countries like Greece and Syria and Colombia.'

'Junkets like those have a bad name now.'

'Banks doesn't exactly smell of roses. MPs call him the Ferret. They say no secret can be buried so deep that he doesn't ferret it out.'

Before returning to his flat, Ian walked round to the offices of the Scotch Whisky Association which were not far away and was given a copy of the Association's latest

168

statistical report. He recognized it as the booklet he had found when he had first opened his father's tuck-box but which later had gone missing. Then he went to the bookshop of James Thin in George Street and bought a copy of *The Spirit of Whisky*, the paperback which Jock Waugh had recommended.

When he reached the flat, Ian found Isobel working at the word processor. He noticed that she must have been to a hairdresser and that her hair was much shorter. The change in style suited her, making her look younger. In Shieldaig she had worn her hair in an untidy cascade falling almost to her shoulders.

On the table near the word processor were several sheets of paper, some screwed up, covered on one side with her small, precise handwriting.

'What are these?' he asked her, pointing to them. 'The fruits of your research?'

'Yes. I never take paper with me to libraries. The librarians are always so helpful. They give me scrap paper, old official forms, and other people's discarded notes, which I can use.'

'Good. I like to see thriftiness in a girl.'

'I'll just finish this page,' she told Ian, 'and then the machine is yours.'

'Just carry on, please. I don't need it.'

She was still wearing slacks, even though

the clothes she had bought the previous day had arrived in boxfuls and were lying around the flat.

'Did you arrange for us to dine with your friends tonight?'

'Yes. We're to go round to their place for a drink first; at about seven, if that's all right.'

'Fine! Don't worry. I'm going to change; put on the warpaint.' She grinned at him and he was surprised again at her ability to read his thoughts.

She continued typing and he watched her for a while. The phrases came easily, he supposed because she had written the opening chapters of the book once already and could remember much of what she had written. From time to time though, she would pause, wondering perhaps whether a phrase could be improved. When she was concentrating she had a mannerism of biting her lower lip and he noticed her lips were full, her teeth small but regular. He became aware that he was beginning to notice things about her features and mannerisms, but told himself that his observations were dispassionate and objective.

'How was your lunch?' she asked, without stopping typing.

'Sinister. They offered me a seat on the board of the West Highland Scotch Whisky Company?'

'Is that the company which owns Loch

Maree distillery?'

'It is, yes.'

'That can't just be a coincidence, can it?'

'I'm sure it isn't. I have the feeling that they may be trying to buy my silence; line me up on their side.'

'Did you refuse?'

'No. That might have made them suspicious, so I said I'd think about it and let them know in due course.'

Isobel stopped working and swivelled her chair round so that she was facing him. 'Exactly how much do you know about this group in which your father and Sandy were involved?'

'Not much. Clearly it is some form of cabal or faction aiming at Scottish independence. Tristram Stewart appears to be the leader, even if he was not the founder and they seem to have named it Scotland Arise.'

'Rather a good name.'

'They've drawn up plans for a provisional government when independence comes.'

'How do you know?'

Ian explained how he had stumbled on the truth about the coded list of telephone numbers which Ballantine had been carrying with him and which he had left at her cottage. Once he knew to whom the phone numbers belonged, it had not been difficult to work out what the letters after each

171

number meant. He showed her the list he had made.

'Does the question mark against the last number mean that you've not identified the person yet?'

'Yes. Because the number is separate from the others it may be that the person to whom it belongs is not a regular member of Scotland Arise, nor of its provisional government.'

'You know nothing about him?'

'Not as yet, but the letters DMO against the name make me believe that he is a soldier, or perhaps an ex-soldier.'

'Why do you think that?'

Ian told her of the recorded message that General Ballantine had posted to his father while he was at Shieldaig. He had referred to the DMO, describing him as 'the biggest bullshitter in the Army'.

'That expression rings a bell.' Isobel thought for a while, frowning. 'Yes, I remember now. Sandy used the same description when he was telling us about the sergeant-major in his regiment. He was still in the Army then.'

'Do you remember the sergeant-major's name?'

'Craig, I believe. Yes, I'm almost certain it was Fergus Craig.'

'Fergus Craig, Frank Chalmers!' Ian exclaimed. 'That's it! He must be the man who rented Mrs Smart's cottage. They say that anyone giving a false name almost always invents one with the same initials as his own.'

'Now, don't get carried away, Ian!' Isobel smiled as an indulgent parent might at an over-excited child. 'It's not much to go on. Anyway having an ex-sergeant-major attached to this Scotland Arise gang may not mean anything sinister. After all the group had no less than two generals.'

'If it was he who threw the petrol bomb into your cottage that's sinister enough.'

'Can we prove it?'

Ian was aware of the implications of her question. Speculation, guesses, were valueless. He had no evidence that the man Chalmers or Craig had been responsible for Ballantine's murder or for setting fire to Isobel's cottage. That Scotland Arise was planning some unconstitutional or even criminal conspiracy would be even more difficult to prove. And yet he had a gut feeling that this must be so.

He would have to work out what he should do next, but could see no reason why Isobel should be involved. Selfishly he had already distracted her too long from her writing. 'You're right. We will probably never be able to prove it. But that's enough of Scotland Arise for one day. I'm off to take a shower and change. This suit was all right for the New Club but it's too dressy for where we're going tonight.'

'Don't be too long in the bathroom, will you. I shall need light-years to make myself even half presentable.'

His shower did not take long, but Ian deliberately spent more time than he usually would have on dressing. He sensed an impatience in Isobel, an impatience which he often felt himself, a desire to get an unwelcome but unavoidable chore finished. In her case that would be the rewriting of what she had already finished once. Writing must offer all the satisfaction of creativity, but there would be little creativity in repetition.

When he returned to the living-room she was no longer writing, and had switched off the word processor and gone to her room. To fill in time as he waited for her, he switched it on again, inserted the disc with Ballantine's papers, and began studying them again. The second page and particularly the numbers and letters at the top of it still baffled him. He looked at them again.

$$60 \times AK47 \times 280 = 16800$$
$$BT \quad \underline{10000}$$
$$6800$$

D 52 477401–477440

B 33 816081–816120
C 28 606141–606180
D 48 522833–522848

The numbers and letters at the top must be a mathematical equation, though Ian could think of no way of solving it. He noticed that the numbers in the list below the equation all had the same number of digits. He had heard of codes in which figures were substituted for letters and if the substitution were made by some simple formula one could decode it on the basis of the frequency of certain letters. The code used here was obviously radically different and more complicated.

He was no nearer solving the problem, and was finding it increasingly irritating, when Isobel returned. She stopped as soon as she was in the room, hesitating diffidently as though uncertain of what reaction her appearance might provoke. Ian was astounded by the transformation in her. She was wearing a black dress, off the shoulder and with a skirt well above the knee, and black tights. Her only jewellery was a single string of costume pearls and long, dangling white earrings. Eye colour, blusher, and lipstick completed the transformation.

'You look great! Fabulous!' Ian told her and then afraid that his compliments might seem too fulsome, he added jokingly, 'I've never seen your legs before.'

'And now you're seeing too much of them. Is that what you're saying?'

'Not at all. They're smashing.'

Isobel smiled but said nothing. Was the smile covering up her embarrassment, Ian wondered. Had the second compliment sounded not insincere but too spontaneous? Again he had the feeling that their relationship was in danger of drifting into uncharted waters. Fortunately, before his doubts could give themselves away in a word or gesture, the radio cab which he had ordered pulled up outside the flat.

In the darkness of the cab Isobel seemed to relax. Or possibly, Ian realized, it was he who was relaxing. She asked him about the friends with whom they would be spending the evening. He told her about Bruce Niven, the outstanding scholar in their school, who had surprised everyone by choosing as a career not the diplomatic corps, nor law, nor even medicine, but journalism. He told her too how Bruce had surprised everyone for a second time by marrying Kirsten, the spoilt daughter of a wealthy and unpopular Edinburgh builder, leader of a wild bunch of young people who had tried to ape the manners and the notoriety of similar groups in Mayfair. Their marriage, as Isobel would see, had not proved the disaster which everyone had expected.

The home of the Nivens was also new; one of a number of small houses, vaguely Georgian in design, that had been built around the docks at Leith. Ian had been saddened to see the historic port of Leith slide into obscurity, but at least the new houses and apartments, restaurants and cafés were reversing the decay and bringing back life.

When they arrived at the house, Bruce reminded Isobel of the time when they had met at Shieldaig, but tactfully did not mention the reason for the meeting.

'You treated me gently,' Isobel told him. 'I appreciated that.'

Bruce grinned. 'What were you expecting? The third degree and rubber truncheons?'

'Well you know what they say about journalists.'

'I do, and most of it is true.'

They all laughed. The two children, aged seven and five, were upstairs being put to bed by the babysitter, and after Kirsten had poured the drinks she took Isobel upstairs to admire them. As soon as they were alone Bruce looked at Ian in amazement.

'Ian! What in the name of Rabbie Burns have you done to that lass?'

'What do you mean?'

'Up in Shieldaig she was, well, a frump. Now she's the sexiest number I've ever seen.'

'I've never seen her dressed up like this

before either. She must have done it for you. I gave you a fantastic build-up.'

'Build-up my balls! Has anyone warned the girl?'

'Warned her?'

'She's sleeping under the same roof as you, is she not? Does she know that Edinburgh mums always lock up their daughters when Ian Blackie is around?'

'Go easy on the lass, Bruce. Maybe her outfit tonight is just part of post-traumatic therapy.'

'What trauma?'

Ian told Bruce about the fire in Isobel's cottage. He gave only the facts, not describing the circumstances or that the fire had followed almost immediately after he had been to see her. He knew though that Bruce would remember their conversation in Kay's bar about the death of General Ballantine. Bruce was not slow-witted and would realize that Isobel's sudden arrival in Edinburgh as Ian's guest could not be unconnected with that event. Fortunately, before he could raise the matter Kirsten and Isobel returned to join them.

They dined at the Vintner's Rooms, a restaurant that had been opened in what had formerly been the premises of a well-known firm of wine and spirit merchants. Before long it was clear that Isobel and Kirsten were going to be good friends. One could sense an instinctive mutual understanding and sympathy flowering. Ian was glad. Not all his girlfriends had been able to strike any form of rapport with Kirsten and Bruce and he had been inclined to blame not the girlfriends, but himself for choosing them.

They talked at first of Isobel's books. In answer to Kirsten's questions, she explained that she had started not as a writer of children's stories but as a reader. She had worked for the BBC radio on a programme in which she had read a series of books written for children.

'What kind of books were they?' Kirsten asked.

'Adventure stories, written for slightly older children. Then I began to wonder whether I couldn't write myself, but for a younger age group. I tried and I was lucky. The third one I wrote was accepted by a publisher.'

'I wish I had heard you on the radio,' Ian remarked.

'You still could. The programme was recorded and I think I have some tapes somewhere.' A fleeting shadow of gloom passed over Isobel's face as she remembered the fire at her cottage. 'At least I had.'

Presently their conversation turned to the subject of Scottish independence. The fury of Scottish Nationalist groups over the supposed insult of the flags to be displayed

179

during the EC summit still dominated the news broadcasts and the press headlines.

'Is it true that the authorities have climbed down over the matter of the flags?' Ian asked Bruce.

'They claim it was not a climb down at all, simply that they had been sent the wrong flags by the suppliers. It's all very childish.'

'Do you not believe then,' Isobel asked Bruce, 'that Scotland should have her independence?'

'I do,' Bruce replied, 'but I don't see it as some noble, romantic ideal. We should look at the subject dispassionately. A sudden severance of the umbilical cord which was wished on us in 1707 would be a disaster. How would we survive?'

'We have our oil.'

'Oh, yes. Scotland's oil!' Bruce replied sarcastically. 'We choose to ignore the fact that the present reserves will not last much beyond the end of the century. And the new wells that are being developed lie nearer to Norway than to Scotland.'

'There's always whisky. Exports of Scotch are massive. The whole world drinks it.'

'Agreed. About sixteen thousand people are employed in the Scotch whisky industry. A useful contribution, but hardly enough to keep our economy afloat. Unfortunately more than eighty, perhaps ninety per cent of the industry is owned outside Scotland; in

England, the States, France, and even Japan.'

'What are you saying? That the time is not ready for independence?'

'I'm saying that if we were to be given it now we could only survive on hand-outs from the European Community. We would be exchanging one master for another.'

'Then what is the answer?'

'We must first rebuild Scotland. At present our best brains belong to Scots living abroad. For generations the most able Scots have left the country. Every English company worth anything is run by Scots. We must bring them back; give them a challenge they could not resist, to rebuild their country.'

Bruce went on to develop his theme. Scotland was a poor country, with few resources. Its key industry, coal, was dead and so was shipbuilding and steelmaking. The future lay in research and inventiveness and more than anything in finance. Scotland was already in the top ten financial centres of the world. It could be lifted up to the top five and made the financial centre of Europe.

'What holds Scotland back is our national inferiority complex,' he added. 'To whinge on about how for years we've been bled by the English only makes other people despise us, especially as it isn't true.'

'You don't have to convert me. I'm one of

the Scots who has come back, remember.'
Ian had done his pupilship with a London
firm of chartered accountants.

Bruce was spreading gloom. There was no
man who Ian would rather have beside him if
it were ever to come to manning the
barricades in Princes Street, but Bruce was
not one to allow sentiment to trample over
logic.

To steer the conversation away from
nationalism, he tossed a question at Bruce,
casually, without any great expectations. 'Do
the initials A.K.4.7. mean anything to you?'

'The Kalashnikov AK47 perhaps.'

'What's that?'

'An assault rifle; favourite of the terrorist
and the most common weapon in the world.'

The Kalashnikov gas-fired rifle, Bruce
explained, had been the standard weapon of
the Soviet Army ever since the 1950s and it
had rapidly replaced all the other rifles and
sub-machine-guns in service with front-line
units of the Communist Bloc armies. The
rifle had been manufactured not only in the
USSR, but in Bulgaria, North Korea,
Poland, and Yugoslavia. The Ministry of
Defence estimated that well in excess of
twenty million AK47s must have been
produced in different parts of the world.

'What makes it so popular?' Isobel asked
Bruce.

'It's compact, robust, reliable, easy to

182

carry, and has a rapid rate of fire, as well as the capacity to fire single shots. Every terrorist of any calibre must have one.'

'Would the IRA have them?'

'I've no doubt they do, though frontal assault is not the Irish way. They prefer to plant their bombs and sneak away.'

'Why are we talking about violence and firearms?' Kirsten gave a little grimace of fear. She may have been thinking of her two small children, asleep safely, she hoped, in their beds at home.

'All this has to do with General Ballantine's murder, has it not?' Bruce asked. 'Have you stumbled on a story, Ian?'

'We're not certain yet,' Ian replied, 'but if we have, I promise that you'll be the first to get it.'

Bruce seemed satisfied with the answer and Ian was glad. He had no wish to be cross-examined, particularly in a crowded restaurant. Moreover any questions Bruce might ask would probably only show how little he knew about the intrigues that had led up to Ballantine's death, that perhaps he was allowing himself to be carried away by imagination.

In a taxi on the way to Dean village, after dropping Bruce and Kirsten off at their house, Isobel said, 'I can't remember when I enjoyed myself more. It was brilliant and your friends are something else, grand

183

people.'

She was sitting close to Ian and he was aware of it; aware of the long, slim legs, her bare shoulders, the large eyes looking at him in the darkness. He said, 'Do you believe that I'm making too much of this business about Sandy's death, finding conspiracies where there are none?'

'I doubt it. That's not your style. You're too sane, too practical.'

'Are you saying I have no imagination?' he asked lightly.

'I hope you have. Otherwise this very expensive dress will have been wasted.' Then as if to show that she was not treating his question too flippantly, she added, 'As to the other business, let's take a look at those papers when we get home.'

In the living-room of the flat they switched on the word processor, found the second page, and looked at what Ian had supposed must be an equation at the top of it.

$$60 \times AK47 \times 280 = 16800$$
$$BT\ 10000$$
$$\overline{}$$
$$6800$$

'I wonder if it might not be an equation at all,' Ian said, 'but simply a statement of money owed? Sixty rifles at £280 each would work out at £16,800. Then "BT" could

184

stand for "bank transfer". When the deal was struck, the IRA had asked for a deposit of £10,000 to be paid by bank transfer and the rest in cash.'

'And Sandy was taking the cash to be handed over at a rendezvous out at sea? In that case couldn't the list of numbers below it not be a code but simply the serial numbers of the bank notes he was taking with him? He might well have wished to take a list just as a precaution.'

Ian pulled his wallet out of his pocket and from it drew a fifty-pound note. 'My God! You're right! This is a fifty-pound note I was given when I cashed a cheque at the bank. The number on it starts with the same letter and has the same number of digits as the first number on Sandy's list.'

They looked at the number at the top of the short list.

D 52 477401—477440

'That might be a batch of notes with numbers in sequence. Forty notes in all.'

Together they made the calculation. Three batches each of forty notes and one of sixteen; one hundred and thirty-eight notes in all.

'Assuming that they were all fifty-pound notes,' Ian said, 'they would amount to £6,800. That proves it!'

'Do you really think he was buying assault rifles?'

'There can be no other explanation. Did you hear about Sean Deeney? The Irishman who phoned Sandy while he was at your place?'

Isobel had not heard the news broadcast, so Ian told her of how Deeney had been shot and killed. The police had believed he had brought his van over from Belfast to pick up a consignment of stolen weapons. The reverse must have been true and he must have been shot after delivering the rifles to Ballantine's outfit.

'But why was Sandy intending to hand the cash over at sea?' Isobel asked.

'I believe the meeting at sea was more than just to complete an arms deal. A message Sandy sent my father suggests that he was hoping the IRA would help in some other way.'

'Does this mean that his group were planning violence?'

'I'm afraid it does.'

'My God! The fools!' Isobel shook her head in disbelief.

'Anyway now that Sandy's dead perhaps they'll abandon their plans. It must have been Sandy's idea.'

'No way! He must have been killed because the others in his group thought he might stop whatever they were planning,

186

betray them.'

'Then what should we do? Tell the police?'

'How can we? All this is mostly conjecture. We've no real evidence. Perhaps if we could work out what those training schedules entailed, we might have a better idea of what they were planning.'

Ian was still sitting in front of the word processor. She leant over him, switched off the machine, and kissed him lightly on the cheek. 'It's late. Let's take a look at them in the morning.'

He walked with her to her bedroom and at the door she stopped to face him. Ian thought she would offer him her cheek to be kissed, but instead she looked at him. 'Last night, you asked me whether there was anything I needed.'

'Is there? Tonight I mean.'

'Only you.'

She was still looking at him, steadily, not smiling. She might just as well have been asking him for a glass of water or a hot-water bottle. There was nothing provocative in her manner, nor anything to suggest that she was only teasing him.

'I'm not sure I know what you mean by that,' Ian said.

'Then why not come in and find out?'

CHAPTER TWELVE

When Ian awoke enough light had breached the curtains to show that morning had almost arrived. Isobel was still sleeping. She lay beside him, her hair just touching his shoulder, her lips slightly apart. Feeling her arm touching his reassured him, for when his eyes first opened he had believed he was waking from a vivid dream. Now, remembering their love-making, he fought back a ridiculous temptation to raise the blanket and look at her nakedness, at the breasts and hips and thighs that had given him so much pleasure.

The pleasure and the ecstasy which it had finally brought had been slow in coming. When they had undressed and he lay down beside her, he could feel her fear. She had returned his kisses awkwardly, complaisant but without passion. Nor had she spoken and did not seem to expect endearments, so he had allowed his fingers to speak for him. Gradually, as he caressed her, her fear had ebbed away and the little cries she began to give seemed more gasps of astonishment than of excitement. Gradually too his own misgivings, the feeling that he might be taking advantage of her, had passed. Then, when passion was spent and she lay with her head touching his shoulder, he had felt her tears running down his arm. She had cried soundlessly and instinct had told him it would be diplomatic to pretend he had not noticed them.

Now, in the morning, as he reflected on what had happened, he realized that below Isobel's façade of brusque good humour lay complexities of character which he would need time to know and understand. Presently she opened her eyes. Recognition came at once and she smiled sleepily. He stroked her cheek with one finger and smiled back.

'Was I quite shameless?' Her voice had a hoarseness which would clear only slowly.

'Why shameless?'

'For seducing you.'

'As you may have noticed I didn't exactly resist.'

'But were you not surprised?'

'To be honest, my love, I was. What you said seemed out of character.'

'It was. My God it was! I wasn't cut out to be a temptress.'

'I don't know about that.' Ian slid one hand below the sheets and touched her breasts lightly.

Propping herself on one elbow, she looked at him seriously. 'It was not just wantonness you know. I had to find out.' Ian said nothing, for he sensed that she would explain herself and any question he might ask would be superfluous. She went on, 'Once I knew you were the only man for me.' She stopped and made a small sound of disgust. 'God, that sounds really naff, doesn't it; romantic rubbish, but you'll understand. I knew you were the one almost at once, that afternoon back at Shieldaig, although I needed a day or two to convince myself. Don't misunderstand me, Ian. I'm not asking for any commitments, nor am I making any. But if there is ever to be a time for commitments I must know that I can offer you'—she hesitated over the word—'everything.'

Ian knew at once what must be in her mind. 'That holiday in the shieling?'

'There you are!' He saw the tears in her eyes. 'I knew you would understand.'

Now she was ready to tell him about the holiday and its still lingering horror, of the boy's insatiable demands, of his coarseness and his violence when she tried to restrain him. Ian was not surprised. So many Scots had a streak of cruelty, the legacy, one supposed, of centuries of savage, bloodthirsty clan warfare. Ian could see the relief in her face as she described what she had told no one before.

When it was done, she was silent for a time. Then she said, 'All these years I was afraid it must have been my fault; that I was—'

'Now you know it wasn't.'

She smiled happily. 'I still can't believe last night. A year or two back I went to the States to do one of those awful lecture tours, promoting my books. In New York they took me up to a bar on the top of a skyscraper, a hundred and seven floors up with a wonderful view. "Windows on the World" they call the bar. Well, last night you opened windows to a new world for me. Sounds silly, doesn't it?'

'If that's true then I find it rather wonderful.'

She leant over and kissed him on his forehead. 'Will it always be as good as it was last night?'

'It will be even better,' he replied smiling, 'wait and see.'

'Do I have to wait?'

She may have been going to say something more, but the words were drowned as he placed his hand behind her neck and drew her mouth down to his.

*   *   *

'Will you be away for long?'

'A couple of days, maybe three. Only as long as it takes to settle what my mother is going to do. I'll need to get back here and start working soon anyway.'

Isobel was sitting on the edge of Ian's bed,

watching him pack the few things he would need to take to Invermuir. He had expected that there might be a change in her manner towards him; no relationship could remain the same after the first intimacy of love. But he could detect no change; no self-consciousness, no demonstrativeness, and, he was relieved to notice, not a hint of possessiveness. She had come into his bedroom to watch him pack only after he had invited her.

'Did I tell you that I met a cousin of mine at the library yesterday?' she asked him. 'Harry Adamson. Only a cousin by marriage, but like almost all of my relations a military type.'

'What was he doing at the library?'

'Studying. Poor Harry. He was in the King's Own Scottish Borderers, but decided there was no future for him in the Army as the regiment is to be amalgamated with the Scots Guards. So he resigned his commission and has got a place at Heriot Watt University as a mature student.'

'That shows enterprise. Good luck to him.'

'He was shattered by Sandy's death; thought of him as a god.'

'Sandy had charisma; there's no doubting that.'

'What impressed Harry was Sandy's vitality. Even after he had left the Army and

192

was in his sixties he was swimming every morning before breakfast at the New Club, exercising in a gym, and hill walking.'

'Harry might not have been so impressed if he had realized that Sandy was getting fit so that he could lead his assault troops in some mad adventure intended to free Scotland.'

'Do you really believe that was what he planned?'

'What else could the AK47s be for?'

'If that's true, it's typical of Sandy. He must have started the whole charade, Scotland Arise, everything.'

'Not necessarily,' Ian said. 'My father could equally well have been the brain behind the conspiracy.'

Behind the façade of a dull, conscientious civil servant, Andrew Blackie had been a romantic, Ian knew that. He could remember his mother, with a rare flash of insight, once describing her husband as the last of the romantics. Rock climbing, sailing, and Munro-bagging had all helped to sublimate his craving for adventure.

'Do you suppose that Harry could tell us anything about Sergeant-Major Craig?' Isobel asked. 'I believe he was in the KOSBs as well.'

'Could be. You might ask the next time you see him.'

'I'll do better than that. I'll ring him at

home. He gave me his number.'

She went to telephone as Ian continued packing. When he had finished and went into the living-room, she was still talking, or mostly listening, drawing out whatever information Harry could give her. As she stood holding the phone she was looking out of the window, through the village and over the bridge across the Water of Leith. The sight of her profile, the stillness of her, the way she smiled, as only Celts can smile, with her eyes alone, had a kind of beauty which Ian had not noticed before and which caught at his emotions. He knew then that he did not want to leave her, but put the thought from him brusquely.

When she had finished her call, she told him, 'Harry says that Craig is out of the Army, living in Glasgow. He believes he's working for the Scottish Soldiers Resettlement Association.'

'That's the outfit of which Sandy was the President.'

'It's all hanging together, is it not?'

'You didn't ask him to describe Craig, I suppose? To make sure it's the same man?'

'Harry would have thought it rather odd if I had, would he not? No, we talked of the Sergeant-Major in a general way, reminiscing about the past, and Harry gave me a description of him, although he probably didn't realize it.'

'That was clever of you.'

'The ability to be devious is one of a woman's most useful gifts. Anyway I am convinced now that it was Fergus Craig who came to see me up at Shieldaig.'

'And burnt your cottage down.'

'Shall we tell the police?'

'We still can't prove anything. In Dingwall I told them we thought a man named Chalmers might have done it. On my way home I'll drop in at the station and tell them that now we think it was Fergus Craig. I doubt they'll be impressed, but we may as well tell them.'

When Ian was about to leave and went to kiss Isobel, she seemed to cling to him, but only briefly. 'Now you'll not do anything foolish when you're up north, will you? I sense that Sandy's friends might be dangerous.'

'Don't worry. I'm one of nature's cowards.'

'I'll not believe that. And let me know when you're coming back.'

'Oh, I'll call you before then, probably tonight.'

He could see her watching him through the window as he drove out of the village. As he crossed Dean Bridge he felt almost guilty, for he had already decided that he would not drive straight to Invermuir and Isobel might well think that what he planned to do was foolish. Before reaching the Forth Bridge he turned off the main road and cut across to join the motorway to Glasgow.

On reaching Glasgow, the first thing he did was to find a telephone directory. No less than eight F. Craigs were listed in it, but the one who had the number 941-1445 lived in Govan. Ian made a note of the address, which was not far from the Rangers football stadium. He also looked up the address of the Scottish Soldiers Resettlement Association, which had its offices near Charing Cross. After leaving his car in a multi-storey car park he found a taxi to take him there.

As the Association was a registered charity, financed by donations and voluntary subscriptions, he had expected that its offices would be modest, even drab and seedy. Instead he found that it occupied the whole of the ground floor in what must have at one time been the home of a prosperous Victorian businessman. A girl with orange hair was sitting in a small office just inside the entrance, tapping on the keys of a word processor without any great enthusiasm.

'Can I help you?' she asked Ian.

'I'm sure you can,' Ian replied, showing her one of his business cards. 'I am anxious to get in touch with the president of your association.'

'We don't have one; at least not at

present.'

'Yes, I heard about the death of General Ballantine. A dreadful tragedy! Has a new president not been appointed yet?'

'Not yet.'

'Do you have a manager I could speak to?'

'There's the director, but he's away just now. His assistant Mrs Morrison should be here, but she's sick. You'll have to make do with me.' The girl was a friendly little soul and Ian sensed that she was pleased to have a visitor to distract her from whatever work she should be doing. 'Sit you down, do.'

'I take it that your association is mainly engaged in finding employment for soldiers who have left the Army.'

'Aye. We've a lot who come in looking for jobs.'

'And can you help them?'

'It's no easy, you ken, but we do our best. And we help them to settle down to civilian life in other ways.'

'What other ways?'

'We send them on management courses, arrange for them to take evening classes. You know the kind of thing. And for them that need it, we even subsidize a holiday for them.'

'A holiday abroad?'

'No. That would cost a bomb. Holidays in Scotland, up in the Highlands mostly. The director's away on one with some of the lads;

skiing up near Fort William. And a while back he was up climbing in Wester Ross. It's all right for some, isn't it?'

'What about you? Don't you ever go on these holidays?'

The girl shrugged and put on a face of comical resignation. 'Little me? You've got to be joking! I'm the wee soul that keeps the place going. Mrs Morrison is away more often than not, especially when the director's no' here. Hangovers. If you ask me she's got a drink problem.'

They chatted for a while longer. The office was well equipped and the machines that Ian could see, word processor, photocopier, fax, and filing cabinets, all looked new and expensive. The Scottish Soldiers Resettlement Association was evidently not short of funds. When he was leaving he asked the girl two more questions.

'What is the name of your director, by the way? I'll need to get in touch with him.'

'Craig. Sergeant-Major Fergus Craig. He still likes us to use his military title. Daft, I call it.'

'And when are you expecting him back?'

'I'm no' very certain. Next week, maybe the week after.'

*　　*　　*

As Ian was approaching Glen Coe, slanting

rain hid the mountains ahead. The day which had been fine when he was in Glasgow had suddenly changed, as it often did near the west coast, and Rannoch Moor, which people described as the most desolate part of Scotland, seemed even lonelier and more forbidding than he had expected. Autumn had lingered longer than usual that year, but winter would start at any time. Perhaps even now the rain was falling on the peaks as snow and by the next morning some of the passes would be closed by drifts.

The roads were empty, allowing him to drive quickly through Glen Coe. Many Scots did the same, shrugging off the little frisson of shame which that scene of infamy provoked. How ironical it was to hear Scottish nationalists complain of English duplicity, when the basest treachery had been that of Scot against Scot in the clan wars of three centuries ago. The massacre at Glen Coe was only one, and not necessarily the worst, example.

He had decided to drive from Glasgow to Invermuir through Fort William on an impulse, not knowing what he would do when he reached it. As recently as twenty years ago one Scottish nationalist group, the 1320 Club, had considered attempting to capture and hold by force some small Scottish town as a means of triggering off a national uprising. Now Scotland Arise was arming a force of volunteers and may well have a similar strategy in mind. That might be the reason why Ballantine had been carrying town plans of Fort William and Inverness in his papers.

He had never been to Fort William before and when he reached it, he found himself laughing at the idea. The town appeared to be no more than a single street running along Loch Linnhe and under the shelter of Ben Nevis. One could see that it would be easy enough for even a small force to capture Fort William and, protected as it was by the loch and the mountains, twenty men with assault rifles should be able to hold it against anything but armour and missiles. What made Ian laugh was the notion that Fort William, once captured, would have any strategic value. The roads leaving from the town led nowhere important and the only industry it possessed consisted of an aluminium works and a whisky distillery. He doubted whether it even had a radio station from which a capturing force could let the world know of its achievement.

He was sure now that the detour he had made had been a waste of time, but as he was driving out of the town he passed the entrance to the distillery. A sign outside the entrance said that visitors were welcome so, again on an impulse, he drove in and parked his car opposite the visitors' centre. As he was getting out of the car a man came out of the centre.

'One of the lassies is showing a party round the distillery just now,' he told Ian, 'but if you care to wait in the centre you could watch our video and she'll be glad to show you round later.'

'Will the lassie be able to answer some questions?' Ian sensed that he was talking to a man who would not be offended by frankness.

'What kind of questions?'

'Commercial rather than technical. Questions about stocks, export sales, and so on.'

The man hesitated and then smiled. 'You'd best come with me to my office. I'm Macdonald, the manager.'

The distillery offices were on the other side of the car park and he led Ian along a passage to what appeared to be the boardroom. Old photographs had been hung on the walls: of the distillery fifty years ago, paddle steamers on Loch Linnhe, and the observatory which had once been on top of Ben Nevis. In a glass cabinet were ranged bottles of the distillery's single-malt whisky at different ages and in different styles of bottle or flask.

'You'll take a dram?' Macdonald asked.

Ian knew that to refuse would be a discourtesy and he allowed Macdonald to pour two whiskies, a generous measure for his guest and a tiny one for himself. The whisky was exceptionally strong, well above normal bottling strength, and Ian added plenty of water to his glass.

'May I ask if you have any special reason for your interest in the commercial side of distilling?' Macdonald asked.

'I may shortly be invited to give a whisky firm investment advice.' Ian explained that he was a money broker. He thought it prudent not to mention that he had also been offered a directorship in that firm.

'It's encouraging to know that a whisky company has surplus cash to invest. The trade as a whole is going through a difficult period.'

'How much whisky would a distillery the size of yours make in a year?'

'Our capacity is in the region of two million litres of pure alcohol a year.'

'Pure alcohol?'

'That's the measurement we have had to use ever since we went metric. Before that it used to be proof gallons. Now everything—production, stocks, sales—is converted to litres of pure alcohol. In the trade we call them LPAs.'

'Let me work this out. A bottle of Scotch is equal to three-quarters of a litre, does it not?'

'In volume, yes.'

'And the strength of the whisky is forty per cent alcohol. So that means a bottle is equal to three-tenths of a litre of pure alcohol.'

'Are you a mathematician?' Macdonald asked, smiling.

'An accountant by training. If I'm right so far that would mean that the amount of whisky you distil in a year here would fill about six million bottles.'

'It isn't as straightforward as that, I'm afraid.'

Macdonald explained that Scotch whisky must by law be matured for a minimum of three years. Malt whisky was usually matured for very much longer, seven, ten or twelve years. Throughout the time it was lying in the warehouses a good proportion of the whisky would be lost through evaporation, which was an essential part of the maturation process. As much as two per cent a year could be lost in this way. In addition to that, a lot of Scotch intended for export was bottled at a strength of 43 per cent.

'Still, your calculations are very roughly correct,' Macdonald conceded.

'And would you say that this is an average-sized distillery?'

'Slightly smaller than average. There are smaller ones but others have a much larger capacity, up to and even more than ten million LPAs. For Scotland as a whole about two and a half million would be the average.'

They chatted on for almost an hour. Ian's interest was fired now and every question he asked appeared to lead to another. He learnt about the vast stocks of maturing whisky that were lying in warehouses all over Scotland. Distillation had to be geared to sales several years ahead and striking the right balance was tricky. More than once in the past, he was told, whisky companies had got their sums wrong. Too much whisky had been produced, triggering off a slump in the industry, during which distilleries had been forced to cut back production and some of them had even closed.

'Don't think that I'm trying to discourage investment in the whisky industry,' Macdonald said. 'Demand for Scotch will never vanish and it's a great business to be in.'

When the time came for Ian to leave, Macdonald walked with him out of the office building towards his car. On the way he asked, 'Is this the first time you have visited a distillery?'

'No. Loch Maree distillery is not far from where my parents stay in Invermuir and I was shown round there by the managing director.'

'Donald Buchanan? He and I trained together.'

Buchanan and Macdonald, it appeared,

had joined the largest whisky company in Scotland several years ago as trainee managers. They had done their training in the same distillery, after which both of them had left the company to take up their present positions.

'David's a bright lad,' Macdonald remarked. 'Like you, he's an accountant.'

'Are you sure of that?'

'Oh aye. Before coming into the whisky business he was articled to a Glasgow firm.'

The clouds of early morning had been blown away by a rising wind and looking up, Ian could see Ben Nevis towering above the distillery. Snow lay on its peak, but not enough for skiing. The previous winter had been unusually mild and were it to be followed by another that would be a disaster for the company who had invested in the cable cars and other equipment needed for skiing, as well as for local hoteliers.

Macdonald had noticed Ian looking up at the mountain. 'It's a grand sight in the sunshine,' he said, 'but in a blizzard the mountain's frightening. And it can be a killer, with hurricanes of a hundred and fifty miles an hour and temperatures way below freezing. In spite of that hundreds of people come to climb it every year.'

'Rather them than me!' Since he was a child Ian had felt an unreasoning fear of heights.

'Mountains bring out the madness in people. We had a couple come in to tour the distillery a short while ago who go round Scotland every year climbing as many Munros as possible. "Munro-bagging" they call it. They've done more than two hundred already.'

'Must be a good way of keeping fit.'

'No doubt, if one doesn't go to extremes. This couple told me that on Chno Dearg behind Ben Nevis, they had seen a group of eight men running up the side of the mountain.'

'Is that so eccentric? I've heard there's an annual race up Ben Nevis itself.'

'Aye, but for trained athletes. They run in summer, wearing singlets and running shorts. These men were fully clothed and, believe it or not, had packs on their backs!'

CHAPTER THIRTEEN

That afternoon when Ian arrived in Invermuir he found that his mother and his aunt were out at a charity tea party, which was being held to raise funds for famine relief in Africa. A small pile of unopened letters lay on a table in the hall. Unlike most of the women he knew, his mother had an aversion to opening letters, believing that more often than not they brought unwelcome news. None of the letters were for him, so he went up to the attic and fetched the book on the Munros of Scotland from his father's tuck-box.

The book, which was illustrated with photographs of some of the more photogenic mountains, described what the authors believed were the best routes for climbing all the two hundred and seventy-seven Munros in the country. It also gave information on the train and bus services by which the mountains could be reached and the accommodation available locally in hotels and guest houses. The Munros were grouped geographically in sections covering the whole of the Highlands; the Cairngorms, Ben Nevis and its surrounds, Glen Coe, Glen Shiel, right up to Assynt and the far north of the country.

After leaving the distillery that morning, Ian had gone to find the hills up which the men with packs had been seen running. Chno Dearg, Stob Coire Sgriodain, and Beinn na Lap were remote mountains tucked away behind and some distance from Ben Nevis. To reach them he had to drive along the road between Spean Bridge and Dalwhinnie and turn down a narrow, winding road to Fersit. When the road ran out he stopped the car in an open space where two other cars were already parked, but there was no minibus and he saw no one running on the mountains.

Now looking at the list of Munros at the back of the book, he saw that all the mountains in the group he had seen had been ticked and so had several others. He had a copy of Ballantine's papers with him and studying it, he found that all the numbers in the Training Schedule corresponded with the numbers of the Munros in the list that his father had ticked. This must mean that the first two weeks of training were to be spent getting the general's assault force fit. Ian could think of no better way of getting men into condition than by making them run up mountains fully clothed and carrying packs.

Checking again with the book, he found that all the numbers put down against the different squads were of groups of mountains not too far distant from Fort William; by Loch Laggan or Glen Coe or the Drumochter hills. This might be because the mountains were easily accessible from Glasgow and Edinburgh, from where most of the men would probably have been recruited. On the other hand it might equally be because the military objective of the force was to capture Fort William.

Ian still found it hard to believe that anyone would wish to capture a town of so little strategic value as Fort William.

Supporters of Scottish independence might see it as having a symbolic value, as one of the garrison forts established by the English in order to subjugate Scotland after the 1715 uprising. Even that required a feat of imagination and if a town were to be captured and held, Inverness would appear to be, marginally at least, a better candidate. That afternoon on the way home from Fort William he had driven through Inverness just to look at the town, which at least had a radio station and was the headquarters of the Northern Constabulary.

The correspondence between the numbers in the Training Schedule and those ticked in the list of Munros could not be a coincidence. Ian was prepared to concede that the first two weeks of a training programme, whether for athletes or assault troops, would be well spent on the mountains, but there was still the puzzle of the last two weeks. It seemed likely that they would be devoted to some form of military training. Trying to guess what it might be, he recalled the old black-and-white films of the war, which even now were shown and reshown on television. Pictures came to his mind of soldiers following each other as they climbed ropes, swung ape-like over pits in the ground, and somersaulted over obstacles in what, he remembered, were called assault courses. Why should not the letters AC stand for assault course? An assault course could easily and quickly be constructed, most probably in the privacy of the estate of a highland landowner. Ballantine had been buying weapons for his force. They would need to be trained in their use. Could WT stand for weapon training? A firing range was also easy to construct.

If he was right the Training Schedule could be a programme intended to bring men up to a high standard of fitness and accustom them to using the AK47s, which most of them would not have fired before. Four weeks was probably the bare minimum needed for this, but any longer period spent training would have made secrecy hard to maintain. That thought triggered off a question which startled Ian. He found the telephone number of the distillery at Fort William from the directory and when he called he was put through to Macdonald.

'You wouldn't by any chance know when it was that your visitors saw those men running up Chno Dearg?' he asked him. Macdonald did not reply immediately. He may have been surprised at the question. So Ian went on, 'Roughly how long ago, I mean.'

'If you hang on I can probably tell you exactly,' Macdonald said. 'They'll have signed the visitors' book in our reception centre.' Ian heard him speaking to one of the guides at the reception centre over the internal telephone. Presently he had the answer. 'It was three weeks ago. Exactly three weeks.'

Ian worked out the implications of the answer as he was putting down the telephone. Scotland Arise's assault force would be nearing the end of its training now, even if it had not already completed it. That would depend on whether they had been seen on the mountain during the first week of the training programme or the second. Once training was finished the force would surely carry out whatever operation had been planned for it as quickly as possible. The success of the operation would depend on a high level of security and every day of waiting would make security more difficult.

A copy of the *Ross-shire Journal* lay by the telephone. The local paper, published in Dingwall, had also been infected by the controversy over the Edinburgh Summit meeting which was due to start later in the week, and the headline over its story read: CLIMB-DOWN OVER FLAGS FOR ROYAL PROCESSION.

Ian stared at it. 'My God!' he exclaimed. 'Of course! That's it!'

What better opportunity could there be for a grandiose gesture in support of Scottish independence, than when the television cameras of Europe would be trained on

Scotland as the Queen opened the Summit meeting?

*   *   *

The copy of *Scotland Betrayed* was in his father's study, where his mother must have taken it in one of her infrequent spells of enthusiasm for tidiness. The room, originally designed by the architect as a morning-room, at a time when such things were considered necessary, had been converted to a study after his father had retired and moved to Invermuir. Ian had always thought of it as a forlorn room, with little in it to remind him of his father, no photographs, no papers, nor any of the small personal possessions which in a study might reflect the character of the person who used it. In his father's case these had all been kept in an old school tuck-box in the attic, which made the study seem even more forlorn and lonely.

Ian had thought of phoning Isobel to tell her what he now knew about the training of Scotland Arise's assault troops but realized that she would no doubt be working on her book and would not wish to be disturbed. He could postpone the call until the evening. In the meantime he opened *Inglorious Failure* and began looking for any clues which might tell him whether the assault was to be made on Fort William or Inverness. With a force of only forty-eight men Scotland Arise could hardly have designs on both towns.

He found two references in the book to plans which had been made, though never carried out, to take and hold Highland towns. The 1320 Club had discussed the possibility of seizing a town on the west coast, either Oban or Fort William. Another nationalist group had drawn up provisional plans for the capture of either Inverness or Aberdeen. On each of the pages where the schemes were mentioned, Andrew Blackie had written his comments in the margin: 'Puerile' and 'Infantile lunacy' against the first, 'Half-witted' against the other.

Ian may have seen the comments when he had glanced through the book previously, but he had taken no particular notice of them. Now they surprised him. How could it be that Scotland Arise, a group in which his father must have been one of the prime movers, should have embarked on a plan which he so clearly scorned? Ian wondered whether perhaps he had been too hasty in concluding that the assault force was being trained to capture a town. There might be other objectives, as for example the capture of an oil rig, which other Scottish nationalist groups were known to have contemplated.

He began going through the book more carefully, not reading the text but his father's annotations, hoping that in them he might find some hint of why Scotland Arise had assembled, trained and armed an assault force.

He found nothing to explain that, but his father's comments were illuminating in other ways. Against a passage in the book which described how British security forces had infiltrated a nationalist group he had written: 'Small groups or cells with no contacts with each other are essential for security.' His remarks at another point in the book showed he believed it was also essential that a group's directing or control body must have plausible reasons for regular meetings which would not arouse suspicion. In the case of Scotland Arise, Ian realized, that requirement may have been met by making members of the group's 'provisional government' directors of two companies. Board meetings of small Scottish companies were unlikely to attract the interest of the security forces.

One chapter in *Inglorious Failure* described in some detail how some of the smaller and more militant nationalist groups had tried to finance their activities by raiding banks and post offices. Andrew Blackie had dismissed these raids contemptuously with just one epithet, 'Rubbish!', and at one point he had added a comment which reflected his own views on the matter, 'Sound funding essential for success.'

214

The comment made Ian think. Scotland Arise was involved in major operations that must be extremely costly. A force of forty-eight men had been assembled and, given the amount of time they had been spending on training, it seemed likely that they were being paid; that they were mercenaries rather than volunteers. The rifles that were being purchased for them were also costly and feeding and transporting them would have been another major expense.

He had another thought. Was the Scottish Soldiers Resettlement Association no more than a front organization for the recruitment and deployment of the assault force? If it came to that, might Endurance Holidays have been created simply to provide the facilities for training the men? Then there was the Tayside Rope Company. He would have liked to know how long the company had been in business. Scotland Arise might have taken a shell of an old company once in the jute business off the shelf and adapted it to its needs. That would not be unusual.

He took a sheet of paper from the drawer of the desk and began jotting down a few speculative figures of what total budget of Scotland Arise would have needed from the time it was formed. Even erring on the conservative side, he kept coming up with a number that had six noughts at the end of it.

Inevitably the next question he asked himself was where the money was coming from. All the members of the provisional government of Scotland Arise were reasonably well heeled, but Ian did not believe that any of them had the kind of money needed to finance an operation of such magnitude.

One possibility was that the funds were being channelled in some way from the West Highland Scotch Whisky Company into Scotland Arise. Ian found it suspicious that the current financial year's accounts of the company had been delayed. The analyst, Jock Waugh, had told him that there had been a remarkable improvement in the company's financial position and had suggested that it might now be shipping malt whisky out to the Japanese. He had no idea of how much money might be involved in such a deal, but the Annual Statistical Review gave him some answers. Malt whisky was being shipped in bulk to a number of overseas countries for mixing with local spirits, but easily the largest market was Japan. One of the diagrams with which the review was illustrated told him that the average value of malt whisky exported in bulk was between five pounds and six pounds per litre of pure alcohol. That did not seem very much and he tried to calculate how much money the West Highland Scotch

Whisky company might be making from this aspect of the trade.

The average annual output of a malt whisky distillery, Macdonald had told him, was some two million LPAs. With its two distilleries, Loch Maree and Loch Torridon, Buchanan's company might be producing double this amount. Jock had also said that the distilleries had continued distilling even in the slump of the 1980s, though no doubt at a reduced rate, and the company must have built up sizeable stocks of mature whisky during this time. If it had shipped say four million LPAs to Japan over the past year or two, that would have brought in at least £20 million. The money needed to finance Scotland Arise could easily have been siphoned off for this purpose and not necessarily illegally.

While he was still in the study, Ian's mother and his aunt returned from the charity tea and were upstairs, changing out of what Ian had mockingly described as their garden-party regalia. As he waited for them downstairs, Ian telephoned Isobel. She told him that she had been working for almost all of the day, stopping only for a cup of tea and a sandwich, and had rewritten almost three thousand words of her new book.

'I'm glad you persuaded me to come to Edinburgh,' she said happily. 'I could never have done that if I had stayed up at

Shieldaig.'

'Is that your only reason for being glad?' he teased her.

'We'll have none of that Barbara Cartland dialogue,' she replied with mock severity, 'not over the telephone anyway.'

Ian told her of his visit to the Soldiers Resettlement Association in Glasgow and to Fort William. He also told her Macdonald's story of the men seen running up Chno Dearg. She listened to what he had to say without interrupting him and without making any comments.

Then she said, 'You may have been lucky that Craig was not in his office when you called.'

'Why do you say that?'

'He's a dangerous man, Ian, and he can be violent, murderous even.'

'Who told you that?'

'Harry. He called me this afternoon and we had a long chat about the Army.'

'I hope you were discreet. Remember he was in the same regiment as General Wreford.'

'Don't worry, my pet. I told him nothing. We were just a couple of old soldiers talking of our Army days.'

'What did he say about Craig?'

Craig, Harry had told Isobel, had almost been court-martialled in the Army for attacking another NCO with a knife and

218

wounding him savagely. During his last years in the Army Craig had trouble with his wife and children and had turned twisted and bitter. Only the fact that he was due to leave the Army within days had prevented him from a court-martial and prison.

'Now he blames the Army for everything,' Isobel concluded.

'Do you suppose he might have murdered Sandy to get his revenge?'

'It's possible, but unlikely, I would have thought.'

'Did Harry tell you anything about General Wreford?'

'Yes, I wormed that out of him as well. Wreford sounds like a clone for Sandy, only without Sandy's charisma.'

'I suppose he has taken Sandy's place and that he and Craig are training this assault force in the Highlands.'

'Will you tell the police?'

'I doubt if they would believe me.'

'Is that the reason, or do you have some hang-up, some sympathy for what Scotland Arise is doing?'

As she so often did, Isobel had guessed what was going through his mind, his ambivalence towards the aims of the nationalist group. It was not only because his father had been so closely involved in Scotland Arise. A grand gesture on the occasion of the Queen's visit to Edinburgh would attract the sympathy of the world for Scotland's aspirations. Ian did not believe that in spite of the AK47s there would be any violence. Who would there be in Fort William or Inverness or on an oil rig to resist even a small force of armed troops? The capture would be only a gesture, a token of Scotland's determination to achieve self-government, to be given up peacefully once the gesture had been made. Even if Ian himself did not believe that independence was a viable option for the future of Scotland, thousands of Scots did. His only uneasiness sprang from the knowledge that Sandy Ballantine must have been murdered in the cause of success, but there would be time for his murderers to be brought to account after the gesture had been made and negotiations for independence begun.

'I understand your feelings,' Isobel said, 'and I share them. But if you intend to warn the authorities, you'll need to act quickly. The summit meeting is due to start the day after tomorrow.'

'I'll sleep on it and call you tomorrow to let you know what I decide.'

'If you ring in the evening, make it late. Harry is taking me out to dinner.'

'Oh yes?'

'He called and asked me out. You don't mind, do you? I feel sorry for Harry. Not only is his career in pieces, but his marriage is breaking up.'

'Of course I don't mind.'

As they were finishing their conversation, Mrs Blackie came downstairs and she must have overheard the end of it. She came up to Ian and kissed him on the cheek.

'I'm so glad!' she said happily.

'About what?'

'You and Isobel. I heard you talking, the way you spoke to her.'

'Now, don't go jumping to conclusions!'

Mrs Blackie smiled. 'I don't know how it happened and I don't wish to know. But just remember this, my lad. When you next bring her home, it's separate rooms.'

'I wouldn't want it any other way,' Ian laughed, and then kissed his mother affectionately. 'You're a clever old thing.'

CHAPTER FOURTEEN

Next morning Mrs Blackie came into the study giving her imitation of how Edwardian ladies might have dusted, if ever they had been obliged to do such a thing. Ian was reading *The Spirit of Whisky*, trying to find out what he could about the export of malt whisky to Japan. He had learnt very little except that the author, like Jock Waugh, disapproved of the trade and thought that the Scots should never have allowed it to begin. Other chapters of the book were more interesting and he had dipped into it at random, reading its stories of the whisky business and of the characters who had enlivened it.

One chapter dealt with smuggling. Scotch, he discovered, was now widely smuggled throughout the world, more popular as contraband than watches, cameras, tobacco, and even than drugs. According to the author of the book, it was smuggled in huge quantities into the Middle East, mainly through Cyprus and into South America through the Caribbean islands of Curaçao and Aruba. He picked up the *Annual Statistical Report*, which had a list of all the countries to which Scotch was exported, giving the volume and value of shipments to them over the past two years. Cyprus, Curaçao, and Aruba all seemed to be importing far more Scotch than their small populations could possibly consume.

'By the way,' he remarked to his mother as she was dusting, 'did you ever tell anyone about Dad's tuck-box?'

Mrs Blackie seemed surprised at the question. 'Tell whom?'

'Anyone. Your ladies of the charity committee, for example.'

'Good Heavens, Ian! What questions you do ask. I may have done. I simply can't remember. If I had, there'd be no harm in it, would there?'

Ian had been worrying about the tuck-box. When he had opened it for the second time, he had noticed that the copy of the *Annual Statistical Report* was missing. Having looked at the copy he had brought back from Edinburgh, he could think of no possible reason why anyone would wish to take it, for it was easily replaceable. What concerned him was how and by whom it had been taken. Could someone have broken into the house, gone up to the attic, and stolen it? It seemed unlikely to the point of absurdity, but he had not forgotten that there had been an attempt to burgle the offices of Carmichael, Campbell, and Duffy in Edinburgh. That had been at a time when the papers his father had left there for Ian were on the premises.

The second time he had opened the box had been on the morning after he and his mother had been taken out to dinner by Nick MacBain. The invitation had been unexpected, made only the same morning at the committee meeting which his mother had attended. Had it been a device to get his mother and him out of the house so someone could come and find out whether his father had left anything in the tuck-box which would betray the plans of Scotland Arise? He remembered too that Mrs MacBain had seemed to know about the tuck-box when she had called to collect his father's trunk. To the best of his knowledge the only other person who knew the box existed was Isobel, for he had told her about it up at her cottage.

Asking his mother any more questions would only alarm her, so he went up to the attic and opened the box again. If the house had been burgled, then surely the burglars must have been looking for something more incriminating to Scotland Arise than a statistical report. And perhaps they had not found it. Once again he spread the contents on the attic floor. Everything, the photographs, the press cuttings, the nationalist posters looked just as innocuous as they had before.

As he was about to put them back into the box, the Walter Scott history caught his attention. Everything else seemed to be connected either with his father's friendship with General Ballantine or Scottish nationalism or both. The book appeared to have no relevance to either. As he glanced through it, he recalled noticing the last time he had handled it that a number of pages were missing. It was scarcely surprising that a book printed sixty years ago should be beginning to fall apart, but when he looked closely at the place where the missing pages should have been, he noticed that they had not fallen out through wear. They had been cut out very close to the spine of the book, probably with a razor blade or very sharp knife. After thinking for a time, Ian made a note that pages 94 to 100 were the missing ones. Then he put the book, the photographs, and everything else back into the tuck-box.

As he was shutting the lid of the box, he heard his mother's voice. 'Ian, you have a visitor,' she was calling from the bottom of the stairs. 'Where have you been? I've called you three times.'

'Who is it?' Ian asked.

'A Mr Montgomerie Banks. He's waiting in the study.'

Montgomerie Banks was short, with thick white hair and the comfortable manner of a man who may have enjoyed too many lunches in the Savoy Grill. His handshake was confident, allowing no possibility that people would not be pleased to see him. He was carrying a red silk handkerchief tucked into one sleeve of his jacket, a habit which one seldom saw now and, Ian had observed, only among older men who had not been able to shake off the affectations of their youth.

'We've never met,' he said. 'I do hope you don't mind my calling on you uninvited.'

'I've heard of you. Isn't your company advising the West Highland Scotch Whisky Company?'

'That's my reason for coming to see you. I had a meeting with Donald Buchanan at the distillery yesterday and spent the night at his home in Strathpeffer. He mentioned that you may be going to join his board.'

'I have been asked to, but haven't decided yet whether to accept the invitation.'

'Quite. You'll need to think about it, of course. Should you wish to know more about the company, perhaps I can help.'

'Frankly, what interests me,' Ian said, 'is what your firm does for the company. As I understand you are parliamentary consultants, are you not?' Banks nodded, so he went on, 'Surely an outfit as small as the West Highland Scotch Whisky Company would not need to be represented at Westminster? Would not the whisky industry's trade association look after its parliamentary interests? I've always heard that the Scotch Whisky Association has a powerful and highly effective lobby.'

'That's true of course, but the whisky business today is dominated by four large multi-national companies. The little men need friends in Whitehall as well as in Westminster.'

Banks told Ian that much of what he did for the West Highland Scotch Whisky Company should be more accurately described as public, rather than parliamentary, relations. That was not

Banks's speciality, but the firm knew enough about the business to be able to help. As an example he described a whisky tasting which he had organized in the Caledonian Club, a London club for exiled Scots, which had been attended by Scottish MPs as well as by the editors of the leading daily newspapers.

'Between you and me,' Banks said confidentially, 'my firm keeps telling me that the work we are doing for Donald isn't economic and that we should be charging a much larger retainer, but I look on it as a personal arrangement. The Buchanan family have been close personal friends of mine for years.'

'An analyst told me that the West Highland Company is doing remarkably well.'

'It is, it is. Malt whisky is on a high just now, particularly in export markets.'

'Is the company shipping bulk malt whisky to Japan?'

Banks looked startled. 'Bless me, no! I wouldn't be associated with any company that did. Selling Scotland's heritage, I call it.'

'I share your view.'

'You've been doing your homework, haven't you?' Banks asked smiling.

'My homework?'

'Checking up on the whisky business.' Banks pointed at the *Statistical Report* which was lying on the desk. 'I couldn't help noticing the report there. That's very sensible of you. And I hope that when you see how well the company is placed, you'll agree to join us.'

Ian had nothing more he wished to say to Banks and had the feeling that the man was not there to be helpful but to check up on him in some way. He would have tactfully brought their meeting to an end at that point, but his mother prolonged it by bringing in coffee for them. As Ian was pouring the coffee, Banks took a silver snuff-box from his waistcoat pocket and sniffed a pinch of snuff up each nostril.

'Tristram Stewart believes this Government is in trouble,' Banks remarked. He too evidently had nothing more to say on the subject that had brought him there.

'Do you agree?'

'I'm not so sure. Tristram is a little out of touch with the Westminster scene. We shouldn't write off Alisdair Buchanan's chances of staying in power. He's proved that he's one of nature's survivors.'

'And when the election comes, how do you think the SNP will fare?'

'Not nearly as well as they think. Oh, yes, they're very bullish now after the regional elections and confident they'll win a majority of the Scottish seats in Westminster, but we've heard all that crap before. Don't get me wrong, Ian. I'm a Scot myself and believe in devolution, but the mob who run the SNP now are second-raters; not worth a fart.'

What Banks was saying sounded plausible enough, but Ian was not convinced that he was being sincere. With his silk handkerchief and his snuff-box, the man reminded him of an elderly actor of the vintage when actors called each other 'old boy' and not 'dearie' and he could no doubt switch from role to role easily and with assurance. If he was involved with Scotland Arise in any way, he was unlikely to give away any secrets.

When finally he left, Ian walked into Invermuir and went to the library. *Tales of a Grandfather* was listed in the catalogue, but the volume which he wanted was out on loan. So he took the current edition of *Who's Who* from the reference shelves and looked up the entry for Major-General Douglass Wreford. Isobel had said Wreford might have been a clone for Sandy Ballantine, and the careers of the two men had run on similar paths. Both would no doubt be described by the tabloid press as heroes. Wreford did not appear to have taken on as many honorary commitments as Ballantine after leaving the Army, but he was a member of the Royal Company of Edinburgh Archers and of the New Club. Ian wondered how he could have been tempted out of a life of seemingly tranquil respectability into the bold adventure of Scotland Arise. Would the offer of the Chairmanship of a small whisky company, with whatever remuneration that might carry, be reward enough?

Since he had the *Who's Who* off its shelf, he thought he might as well look up the entry for Tristram Stewart and found that it was a great deal longer than that for Wreford. Stewart had held three or four minor Government posts in different departments before being appointed Minister of State in the Scottish Office. When he lost that, he had given up his seat in the House of Commons by not standing at the last election. Earlier, as a back-bencher, he had served on a number of Select Committees, mainly those concerned with agriculture, fisheries, and tourism, all subjects of special interest to Scotland. He had also been a member of the Anglo-Brazilian and Anglo-Colombian inter-parliamentary unions. His directorship of the West Highland Scotch Whisky Company was not mentioned, which must mean that he had left the board before the current issue of *Who's Who* had been published. Ian was surprised, for he had formed the impression that Stewart's resignation had been much more recent.

On his way home from the library he called at a bookshop and bought a copy of Number 52 in the Landranger series of Ordnance Survey maps. A small sketch on the cover of the map showed that it covered an area north and west of Perth. There would be few Munros in that part of Scotland, he knew, and none of those which were listed in the training schedule of Scotland Arise. He wondered why his father had kept it in the tuck-box.

When he reached home he phoned his flat in Edinburgh. Isobel could not have been there, for after a few seconds he heard his own voice on the answer-phone. As always the sound of its too controlled, impersonal message irritated him. He waited until the message was finished and then left his own message for Isobel.

'This is Ian. If you have time this afternoon could you possibly go to the library and look up something for me. It's a book which was in my father's tuck-box; *Tales of a Grandfather*, by Walter Scott. Pages 94 to 100 seem to have been cut out of my father's copy. I'm curious to know why. It may be important so I'll call you back.'

He would have liked to finish the message on an affectionate note, but felt that any endearments might sound forced and artificial. So he ended by saying, 'Hope you enjoy your dinner. I'll speak to you soon.'

*   *   *

Over lunch Ian, his mother, and his aunt,

discussed plans for the future. He did not think his mother should live alone in Invermuir and she made it clear that she had no wish to go and stay with him in Edinburgh, even for a short time. Ian was sure she felt that way simply because she did not wish to intrude on him and Isobel. His flat had three bedrooms, but his mother would be afraid of being in the way and spoiling their new and possibly still fragile relationship. Finally they hit on a solution. His aunt would sell her own house and go to live with Mrs Blackie. She was a widow with only a modest pension and the proceeds from the sale of her house would enable her to live much more comfortably than she did now.

'I'll only agree,' his aunt said, 'provided your mother and I share the expenses of running this house.'

'That won't be necessary.'

'I insist.'

'I knew you would,' Ian said with an exaggerated sigh of resignation, 'you two sisters have the same stubborn pride.'

'And why should we not have?' his mother demanded. 'We are Scots, you know.'

The two women then began to talk about some alterations which they would like to make to the house, which would be small enough but need a builder to make them. Ian could see that his mother was delighted at the thought that her sister would be living with her. They had always been close.

'The alterations will be to your advantage too, for the house will be yours eventually; a home for you and your family,' Mrs Blackie told Ian, and he knew that in her imagination he was two-thirds of the way to being married and giving her the grandchildren she had always wanted. He could understand how she felt because she had married relatively late in life, had only two children, and the eldest, Ian's sister, had died of meningitis before she was eighteen.

After lunch he drove to the police station in Dingwall. During their phone conversation the previous evening he had sensed that Isobel, although she had given him no advice, believed he should tell the police what he knew about Scotland Arise and its plans. The visit of Montgomerie Banks that morning had inclined him to the view that he must. For a reason that he could not identify, the visit had made him feel uneasy. The reasons Banks had given for coming were unconvincing and throughout their conversation Ian had noticed that behind the façade of bonhomie his eyes had been watchful. Had he come to spy on Ian, to find out how much he knew of Scotland Arise and whether he was in a position to frustrate them?

Another cause for Ian's uneasiness was the

tuck-box. If it had been rifled then Nicholas MacBain was the only person who could have arranged it. MacBain too had been his father's doctor, had signed the death certificate. The thought that his father's death might not have been through entirely natural causes, which had hovered in the recesses of Ian's mind ever since the fire at Isobel's cottage, had finally emerged now and was taking shape. Any sympathy which he had felt for the conspiracy that was being planned by Scotland Arise had evaporated.

As he drew near Dingwall, he could see the monument to Sir Hector Macdonald standing on a hill above the town. There had been questions about Sir Hector's death too. People still believed that he may have been assassinated to rid the British government of an embarrassment. Books had been written defending him and attacking the authorities.

Ian was kept waiting at the police station for almost an hour until Inspector Dunlop, who had interviewed him on his first visit, was free and could see him.

'Are you here in connection with the fire at Miss Gillespie's home?' Dunlop asked.

'Not directly, no.'

'I may as well tell you that we have decided it was caused by an accident.'

'An accident?'

'An explosion. She used Calor gas in the cottage.'

234

'Do you have any proof of that?'

'Proof, no, but that's what the experts believe. So we have decided that we need not continue our investigations.'

'You're making a mistake, Inspector. Events which have happened following the fire have convinced me that General Ballantine's murder was part of a conspiracy.'

'What conspiracy?'

'One planned by a Scottish nationalist organization.'

Dunlop looked at Ian with disbelief. 'You're joking, Mr Blackie, of course.'

'On the contrary. What is happening is extremely grave; a threat to national security.'

'All the nationalist organizations are known to us. If there was any truth in what you say, we would have heard about it.'

'Will you at least listen to what I have to say?'

'Certainly. That's my duty.'

As he started to tell Dunlop about Scotland Arise, Ian was conscious that he was doing it badly. Not only was his story short on facts and overloaded with assumptions, but it must have seemed incoherent. He began by saying what he knew about General Ballantine's death, which was a mistake for he had told Dunlop that before. There was nothing to add, except the name of Sergeant-Major Craig, and even now Ian had no proof that Craig had actually placed the bomb on board Ballantine's boat and detonated it.

'Mr Blackie,' Dunlop interrupted him, 'you told us all this before. We checked your allegations at the time and could find nothing to substantiate them.'

Ian's account of the papers that Ballantine had left in Isobel's cottage must have sounded equally unconvincing. Why had she not told Ian about them during his first visit? Why had she made a copy of the seemingly meaningless numbers and letters on her word processor? By what extraordinary stroke of good fortune had she taken the disc with her to the inn on the evening when the cottage was burnt down? Ian watched the cynical incredulity in Dunlop's face grow as he was talking.

'If what you say is true, Mr Blackie, the money to pay for the rifles must have been with General Ballantine on his boat. If the IRA were not paid, why should they have delivered the rifles?'

'More cash could have been raised and paid when the rifles were handed over.'

'You are saying that the man Deeney must have brought the rifles to Scotland in his van. No money was found on him when he was shot and killed.'

Dunlop's disbelief turned into amusement

236

when Ian described how Scotland Arise's assault force was being trained in the mountains and the purpose for which they were to be used. 'Are you saying that the plan is to capture Fort William or Inverness?'

'It looks that way,' Ian replied cautiously.

'For what possible reason?'

'To make a political gesture.'

Ian was about to explain that the gesture was to coincide with the opening of the summit meeting in Edinburgh, when he became aware that throughout the time that he had been speaking Dunlop had not made a single note. The pad which lay on his desk in front of him remained blank. The previous time he had been interviewed by Dunlop a sergeant had been present and had taken notes. The difference, Ian supposed, was that on the last occasion he was being interviewed as a possible suspect in a case of arson, but now he was being treated as a harmless crank. He began to lose his temper.

'Are you not making any record of what I'm telling you?' he demanded. 'Some of the facts could be extremely important.'

'What facts have you given me? All I've heard is a theory and a most implausible one at that.' Dunlop was clearly growing impatient. He may have been wanting to get home for his tea. 'When you have finished we'll ask you to make a written statement in the presence of a sergeant.'

'You'll take no action then?'

'We will decide whether any action is needed when we have the statement. The decision will be one for my superiors in Inverness to take.'

'In that case I'll make no statement. Why should I waste my time?'

'Just as you please, Mr Blackie.'

On the drive back to Invermuir, Ian felt no regret for having lost his temper and walked out of the police station. Once he had realized the futility of talking to Dunlop, to continue talking would have been a waste of time and time was becoming crucial. The heads of state of the European Community had already arrived in Edinburgh for the summit meeting which was to open tomorrow. Any gesture that Scotland Arise was planning must be made within the next two days when the attention of the world was focused on Scotland. He decided that he would do now what he should have done earlier and tell Bruce Niven everything. Bruce would have the resources to find out what Scotland Arise was planning. Even more important, he would be listened to, by the police and the security service. The authorities would not dismiss him, as they had done Ian, for a harmless crank.

On the drive home the weather worsened. Sleet began to fall, slanting across the road densely enough to reduce visibility and make the windscreen wipers almost ineffective. This could be heralding the arrival of winter at last, but Ian was not certain whether it would hamper the operations of Scotland Arise or assist them.

When he arrived home he telephoned Bruce's home number and Kirsten replied. Bruce was in Glasgow, she told him, and likely to be late in returning. He had been sent to cover a story, but she did not know what the story was. Ian asked her to tell Bruce to phone him in Invermuir, no matter how late he got home. Then he rang his flat and, knowing that Isobel was dining out, was not surprised to get the answer-phone. He left a message on it for Isobel, asking her to contact Bruce if she could and to tell him everything they knew about Scotland Arise.

Satisfied that he had done as much as he could, he sat down to supper with his mother. They were eating early so that his aunt and mother could watch one of their favourite TV programmes. Earlier in the evening they had been watching a news programme and were able to give Ian a detailed account of the Queen's arrival in Edinburgh, and describe how the heads of state had been piped off their aircraft at Edinburgh airport. Thousands, even millions, of other Scots, Ian reflected, must be getting the same pleasure out of the occasion and its ceremonial.

The phone rang just as they were leaving the table and Mrs Blackie went to answer it. 'It's for you Ian,' she said, 'a man. He wouldn't give his name.'

'Blackie?' A man's voice said roughly as Ian put the instrument to his ear.

'Yes. Who's that?'

'Never mind. Just listen to what I'm going to tell you. We're holding your bird, Isobel Gillespie, here and unless you do what we tell you you'll not see her alive again.'

This is a joke, Ian told himself and wondered who might be playing it. He waited, for he was sure there was more to come. The man at the other end of the phone grew impatient. 'Did you hear what I said?'

'What do you want?'

'You've to come and join your bird here so we can keep an eye on the two of you. Just for a day or so. Do as we say and neither of you will get hurt.'

Ian thought quickly. 'How do I know that you have Miss Gillespie there?'

'I'll put her on the line.'

Moments later Ian heard Isobel speak. 'It's true. They've captured me!' The voice sounded forced but Ian had no doubt that it was Isobel's. After a pause she went on urgently, imploring, 'Do as they say, please.' Another pause. 'Come quickly!'

'Isobel!' Ian began.

240

'That's enough.' The man had the phone again. 'Are you coming or do we have to kill her?'

'Where are you?'

'We're holding her in the cottage at the back of Ardnadaig. You've been to the place.'

'Mrs Smart's place?'

'Aye, that's the one. Come at once and come alone. Don't bring anyone with you and don't try to tell the police. You'll be watched all the way. If you're not here in ninety minutes we'll rape the bird and then cut her throat.'

CHAPTER FIFTEEN

The weather had changed, the sleet shower stopping as a fierce wind scoured the night sky of clouds. Later, perhaps in early morning, the wind would drop, the clouds return, and there might be snow, enough to make some of the roads impassable. That would be the first sign that winter had finally arrived.

As he drove along the empty roads, Ian was not conscious of the weather. When he had put down the telephone and even as he left Invermuir, he had still been incredulous, only half-willing to accept that the call had not been a hoax. For a time he had even wondered whether it might not be the work of Bruce, who had been a tireless practical joker as a boy. Perhaps he and Isobel together had devised this elaborate spoof.

Then he remembered Harry Adamson. Harry had met Isobel by chance in the library at Edinburgh. Or had it been by chance? Harry had been in the KOSBs, the same regiment as General Wreford. Harry had invited Isobel to dinner that evening. He might easily have called at the flat earlier that evening to collect her. Once he had her in a car it would not have been difficult to kidnap her and drive north. Her voice had sounded strained. Might they have drugged her?

It seemed to Ian that the pieces were falling into place. By questioning Harry about Sergeant-Major Craig, Isobel had revealed how much she and Ian knew about Scotland Arise. How much more might she have unwittingly told him? By now the provisional government may well have learned of Ian's visit to the Soldiers Resettlement Association. And only an hour or two ago he had been talking to the police in Dingwall. That had been the supreme idiocy. He should have remembered that on his last visit to the station Graeme Ross had been there. Ross would have no doubt heard from the Dingwall police of how Ian had been to see them that afternoon.

Only one thought was reassuring. Although the members of Scotland Arise had shown that they were ready to use violence to prevent their plans being betrayed, it appeared that they did not intend to kill Isobel or him. That made sense too. They could be kept in a safe place, prevented from telling the authorities what they knew or suspected, until after the coup, whatever that might be. Once it was over, Scotland's aspirations would be paraded before the world and the British government humiliated. No one would be interested then in anything Isobel or he might say.

He drove as fast as he safely could in darkness, impelled not by fear but by the fearful pleading in Isobel's voice. The single-track road between Kinlochewe and Loch Torridon slowed him down, for it was still muddy from the rain and sleet that had fallen. Above him the moonlight was reflected in the snow on the highest peaks. 'The new soft-fallen mask of snow upon the mountains and the moors,' he said aloud, and marvelled at the incongruity of reciting poetry at a time like that. Perhaps poetry was not just a distraction but an analgesic to calm his anxiety. A few minutes later, as he rounded a bend in the road, he saw lights directly in his path, a car's headlights with the blue lamp of a police car above them. As he approached them a man with a torch waved him down to stop. He saw then that there were two policemen, both wearing yellow fluorescent jackets over their tunics.

'Where are you heading for, sir?' one of the policemen asked when Ian had stopped his car and wound down his window.

'Ardnadaig.'

'Your name, sir, please.'

'Blackie. Ian Blackie. I've come from Invermuir.'

'I'm afraid the road ahead is blocked, sir,' one of the men said. 'A truck carrying ballast collided with a petrol tanker.'

'Can't one drive round the obstruction?'

'On these roads? Impossible, I'm afraid, sir, and there's a risk of fire too.'

'But I have to get through.'

'Then you'll need to use that road.' The man pointed to where some fifty yards ahead there was a circular blue sign of the type used when roads were being repaired. A large white arrow on the sign was pointing to the left. 'Just turn down there, sir, and follow the track. It's one the forestry people use, but wide enough. Follow it for about a couple of miles and you'll see another track off to the right which will lead you back to the main road.'

'Thank you, officer.'

'Mind how you go. Watch out for deer.'

The surface of the track into which Ian had been directed was better than he had expected, but the track was narrow and twisting, with a sharp drop into a burn on its left. He drove with full headlights, which made grotesque shadows of trees and from time to time picked out the figure of a sheep. Impatient, remembering that Isobel was in danger, he forced himself to drive slowly.

Suddenly he cursed. Ahead of him, stretched out in the middle of the track was a sheep, sleeping as sheep do in a kneeling position with its head on its knees. He sounded the car's horn, hoping to rouse it, but the creature did not stir. He had stopped the car and was reaching to undo his safety belt, when another sheep came on to the track from the right and moved with a sheep's fastidious, mincing walk towards the sheep lying on the ground. Ian wondered for an instant whether it might be a lamb searching for its mother and then remembered it was not the season for lambing.

Then as it reached the sheep on the track, both sheep seemed to explode. The blast of the explosion hit the car, hurling it backwards. Ian felt his head thud against the restraints at the back of his seat. Then came another much louder thud, the crunch of metal buckling as the car struck a tree behind it. He knew he was stunned but did not lose consciousness. The windscreen had not shattered, but was covered in wool, splashes of blood, and what might have been entrails. Presently, after one final delayed noise of creaking metal, came silence; only a moment of silence before the beating of wings and frightened cries of birds leaving the trees.

Ian felt numb, but when he tried to move the pain was hideous. The door on his side of the car had sprung open in the crash and he clambered out, stumbled when he tried to stand and had to support himself against the buckled car. He was not too numb to think.

A booby trap; a booby trap in a dead sheep, a sheep that had been killed, filled with explosives and planted carefully in the track to look as though it were sleeping. In wars retreating armies left booby traps behind them to kill careless pursuers. Terrorists in Ireland used booby traps. The plastic explosive would be easy to obtain and was easy to handle. To his surprise he felt no fear.

The police must have sent him down the track knowing that the booby trap was there. They had asked for his name to make sure they had the right man. Were they police and had the road signs been genuine? Police cars, uniforms, and road signs could all be stolen.

So it had been a deliberate plot to kill him and it had failed. Ian realized that was no cause for complacency. Surely the two men would check to see whether the booby trap had worked? It would take them no more than a few minutes to drive down the track and make sure. If he were alive still and injured in the car, they would pour petrol over it and strike a match.

Now fear did come. He must get away from the car, hide among what trees he could find—and what then? Make his way back up to the road and head for Ardnadaig? It must be all of ten miles. He realized that he was not thinking straight. Why should he go to Ardnadaig? Isobel had been the bait for the trap. He had no reason to believe that she was in Ardnadaig. They could be holding her anywhere, if all they wanted was to make sure she remained silent. If on the other hand they were determined to guarantee her silence as well as his, she might already be dead. The thought made him flinch.

He left the track, not to the right where anyone following him might think he would go, but to the left, wading through the burn and keeping behind what cover he could find. He planned to make a wide semicircle, keeping away from the track and aiming to rejoin the main road well down in the direction of Kinlochewe. The going was rough for the sky had clouded over now and once he was clear of the trees, it was difficult in the darkness to pick a path in the heather between the rocks. The ground was wet and every now and then he would slip unexpectedly into several inches of water.

At one point he thought he saw the lights of a car as it nosed down the track towards where the booby trap had exploded, but he could not be sure. When eventually he reached the road and looked down it in the direction of Loch Torridon, he could see no police car and no road signs.

The best he could hope for was that the men who had ambushed him had written him off as dead and returned to wherever they had come. He set off towards Kinlochewe which would be the nearest place where he would find a phone box from which he could telephone for a taxi. There were taxis in Invermuir, though he would have to call a driver who knew him. No one would drive out several miles at night to pick up a stranger from a phone box.

He had walked only a hundred yards or so when he heard the sound of an engine approaching from behind him. Quickly he scrambled off the road and hid from its lights behind an outcrop of rock. It was not a police car that went past but a delivery van. Not long afterwards another vehicle came up and he saw that it was a private car, a BMW, not long registered. He realized that it might take him hours to walk to Kinlochewe. The only alternative was to take a chance and try to thumb a lift. Some kind soul might take pity on a man walking along the road at night and he could only hope that it would not be the men who had ambushed him.

To maximize his chances whenever he heard an engine behind him, he looked back and tried to guess what kind of vehicle it was. The first to pass was a truck, too heavy for those roads, and he was not surprised when the driver ignored his thumb. The second was a Mercedes which also did not stop. The farmers of the Highlands were prospering under the Common Agricultural Policy, he thought morosely.

The lights of the third vehicle to approach seemed faint and were flickering slightly as though they had been shaken loose from their mountings after years on Highland roads. Ian flagged it and the driver stopped and wound down his window.

'Are you in trouble?' he asked.

'My car is off the road and smashed up.'

'Where are you heading for?' the driver asked, and when Ian told him he said: 'I'll drive you there.'

They drove in silence for a while. The man was probably a crofter, Ian decided, and not a great conversationalist, but trustworthy and courteous. These were the real Scots, and it was they who should be allowed to decide how the country should be governed, not second-rate politicians who only used nationalism to inflate their self-importance, nor the malcontents, nor the frustrated soldiers.

'You'll not be staying in Kinlochewe?' the man asked him.

'No, in Invermuir.'

'I thought not. And what will you do when I drop you in Kinlochewe?'

'Telephone for a taxi.'

'Man! Who'll come out to fetch you at this time of night? I'll drive you home.' When Ian tried to protest the man went on, 'Och, once you have the wee car started it's nae bother to keep going. Though she's no' so willing to start these days.'

If it had been anywhere but the Highlands, Ian would have offered to pay for the petrol, but there was no way he was going to repay a favour with an insult. Outside his parents' house they exchanged the few words that can pass for a conversation among Highlanders, but the man kept the engine running. 'Just as a precaution, you understand,' he explained.

Mrs Blackie was still up although her sister had gone to bed. When she saw Ian come into the house, dishevelled and with the bottoms of his trousers and his shoes soaked and plastered with mud, she was not as shocked as he had expected.

'You're as bad as your father,' she complained. 'What have you been up to this time? Hill walking? Fishing?'

To have told her that he never fished or walked the hills, even by day, would have taken too long, so Ian explained that his car

250

had been damaged in an accident. His mother did not seem surprised at that either.

'You'll not be immobile though,' she said, 'your father's car is still in the garage. Now go upstairs and change, for Heaven's sake!'

'I must telephone first.'

'Yes do. Isobel called just now and asked for you to ring her back.'

Ian fought back alarm. 'Did she leave a number?'

'Yes. She's dining out in Edinburgh.'

Ian choked back his emotion, disguising it with a sharp laugh which made his mother look at him sharply. 'Edinburgh? Are you certain?'

'That's what she said. Why should she be lying?' Mrs Blackie looked at Ian suspiciously. 'Have you been drinking?'

The relief which coursed through Ian was as powerful as the horror which had gripped him when he thought her life was in danger. What he had thought to be a hoax and had become a nightmare, had suddenly slipped back into the world of reality. He dialled the number his mother had given him and had to wait for a full two minutes before Isobel was brought to the phone.

'Where are you?' he asked her.

'In the New Club. Harry brought me here for dinner. He's a member.'

'Listen,' he told her, 'as soon as you finish your dinner get the porter to order you a taxi and go straight to Bruce's house in Leith. I shall phone Kirsten and tell her to expect you.'

'But why?'

'Wait in the club for the taxi to arrive and go straight to Leith. Don't let Harry get in the cab with you.'

'How can I stop him if he wants a lift?'

'Make some excuse and spend the night with Bruce and Kirsten. Please, darling, do what I say.'

Isobel did not answer at once. Ian could almost hear her thinking, working out what must have provoked his entreaties and the urgency in his tone. 'They've tried to kill you, haven't they?' she said at last.

'Yes. I'll tell you about it soon.'

'How soon?'

'I'm driving down to Edinburgh directly.' Ian went to put down the phone and then remembered he had something to ask her. 'By the way, why did you leave a message for me to call you?'

'To tell you that I looked up the Walter Scott book and checked the missing pages.'

'Did they mean anything?'

'Most of it was pretty boring. Folksy history and not very well written. All about the Scots fighting off the English in the reign of Edward the Second.'

'Is that all?'

'There was one passage.' Isobel's tone

changed and he sensed that she was holding back her excitement. 'Hang on. I copied it out. I'll read it to you.'

'Wait! Can Harry overhear you?'

'Of course not! I'm in one of those phone booths outside the dining-room. Why do you ask?'

'Just a precaution. Read it, please.'

Isobel began reading.

So while Randolph was considering what was to be done, there came to him a Scottish gentleman, named Francis, who had joined Bruce's standard, and asked to speak with him in private. He then told Randolph that in his youth he had lived in the castle of Edinburgh and that his father had then been keeper of the fortress. It happened at that time that Francis was much in love with a lady, who lived in a part of the town beneath the castle, which is called the Grassmarket. Now, as he could not get out of the castle by day to see his mistress—

'God in heaven!' Ian interrupted her. 'They're planning to take Edinburgh Castle!'

CHAPTER SIXTEEN

Edinburgh Castle, thought to be impregnable on its steep, rocky perch, had been recaptured from the English in 1313 by a small band of armed Scots. They had climbed Castle Rock by night, following a secret route known only to one of their number, who had discovered it himself when he had been a member of the Castle's garrison. The guard, taken by surprise, had been easily overcome.

Ian remembered the story, and as he drove south in his father's car could not fight back a grudging admiration for the leaders of Scotland Arise. Capturing the Castle at a time when the Queen was entertaining her guests in Holyroodhouse just down the Royal Mile would be a daring and spectacular feat. But could it be done? Security in and around Edinburgh would be at its highest, impenetrable one would have thought. The IRA had been active all summer in Britain and everyone was expecting that they might strike again. For weeks every Irishman in Edinburgh would have been kept under close surveillance and a number had been unceremoniously asked to move on. Anti-terrorist legislation was even more elastic than its opponents believed.

Most of the pieces of the puzzle which he and Isobel had been trying to solve fell into place now; the purchase of assault rifles, the training of men on mountains, the retaining of consultants to generate the maximum media publicity when the Castle was taken, the massive financial investment. Only one thing still puzzled Ian. Why had the leaders of Scotland Arise suddenly decided that he must be eliminated? They could have killed him more easily at any time. He could not help thinking that it must in some way be connected with the visit of Montgomerie Banks to Invermuir that morning. What had Banks seen which might have convinced him that Ian knew too much?

He had also been wondering about how he had been trapped into setting out for Ardnadaig. At first he could not imagine how he had been deceived into thinking it had been Isobel's voice he was hearing. Then he recalled that Isobel had once read stories on radio and said she had tapes of the recordings. If she had been able to get tapes, so could others have done. Now he understood why her voice had sounded strained, why she had said that she had been 'captured'. The word had sounded out of place and rightly so.

His father's car, although no longer new, was in good running order but the petrol tank would need refilling for a journey to Edinburgh. Knowing that there were few petrol stations on the road south, Ian turned into Inverness after crossing the Moray Firth and stopped at the first garage. While driving he had noticed that dust had gathered on the windows of the car, not surprisingly for it had been standing idle for some weeks. So, after filling up with petrol, he opened the glove compartment, hoping he might find a duster or rag there which he could use to clean them. Instead he found a large brown envelope, stamped and ready for posting and addressed to Carmichael, Campbell, and Duffy in Edinburgh. Inside the envelope was a smaller one which had his own name on it.

This could only be another instalment of the evidence his father had been collecting to prove that Ballantine had not been killed by the IRA and which he had not been able to post before he died. Ian did not bother to open the smaller envelope. Ballantine's death had been overtaken by events and as part of a larger scenario was now only of secondary importance. He could open the envelope later but meantime he must get to Edinburgh as quickly as he could.

As he drove down the A9 he tried to place other pieces of the puzzle. Hill walking or even running would not be effective training for climbing Castle Rock in Edinburgh. Experienced climbers would be needed for the assault and even they would need practice. Then he remembered that in the Training Schedule the letters RC had been marked against one squad and must stand for rock climbing.

It all seemed to make sense, and if the assumption was correct only eight men, headed perhaps by General Wreford, would make the assault of the castle. Eight men, he supposed, could overrun the castle's guard if they were to climb over the wall behind the gatehouse and surprise them. The rest of Scotland Arise's force would meanwhile take up positions near the entrance to the Castle, hiding in the narrow wynds that led off the Royal Mile. Once the guard had been disarmed, the support force would be allowed through the gate and the Castle would be taken. The beauty of the scheme was its simplicity and in fact it was the only way, short of bombardment, to capture the Castle. One could scarcely launch an armoured attack up the Royal Mile.

The only problem would be one of timing. Obviously the walls could only be scaled at night, but for most of the night the Castle and the Rock were floodlit. The attack would have to be made after the lights were switched off, for even if the guard did not see the climbers on the Rock people in Edinburgh, insomniacs or late-night revellers, would and raise the alarm.

As he drew near Pitlochry, he remembered that when he and Isobel had followed the scenic route to Perth two days previously they had seen a number of climbers leaving a minibus on the road just north of Dunkeld. The minibus had belonged to Endurance Holidays, a subsidiary of the Tayside Rope Company. Could the men have been Squad F of Scotland Arise's assault force practising rock climbing?

Realizing that it was time for the broadcast news, he turned on the car radio and was in time to catch the first item.

'Just two hours ago,' the announcer was saying, 'a bomb exploded in a Glasgow shopping centre. Sufficient advance warning had been given by the IRA, who planted the bomb, for the centre to be cleared and nobody was killed in the explosion. Eight people were taken to hospital with minor injuries. The shopping complex, in Princes Square, has been admired throughout the world for its innovative design. It is estimated that the bomb has caused millions of pounds worth of damage. The area and the streets leading to it have been closed by the police.'

Ian guessed that the bombing must be the diversion which the IRA had promised to make to assist Scotland Arise. It would divert attention from Edinburgh. Police would be rushed to Glasgow; searches would be begun for more bombs and for the bombers.

The Ordnance Survey map he had bought in Invermuir was in the car, together with *Inglorious Failure* and *The Spirit of Whisky*. Leaving the A9 he pulled in to the side of the road, switched on the car's interior light and opened the map. Its contours showed that a short distance from the road where he had seen the climbers the land rose sharply in what might well be rock faces.

If he was right, this would be the last week of the assault force's training. It might even be there that evening, practising climbing in darkness. He drove through Pitlochry, which was drowsy now, with all the shop windows in darkness and not even laughter coming from the hotel bars that were still open.

He found the spot where they had seen the minibus without difficulty, but there was no minibus there now. Fifty yards along the road the grass verge was wide enough to take a car, so he parked there and set off through the trees to where he calculated the rock faces must be. The copse of trees was denser than he had thought, but there was a rough track between them. Tyre tracks on the ground showed that the track had been used and recently.

He had to walk for more than five minutes before he found the rock faces and realized that the place was ideal for anyone who wished to climb without being observed from the road. He had not believed that there would be any cliffs or rock faces so near at hand. That thought had scarcely taken shape in his mind when he saw the minibus parked where it was partly hidden by a shelf of rock.

This time there were two tents beside it; a large circular one and a smaller rectangular one. A lamp was hanging in the larger tent which threw the shadows of the people inside on the walls. Six, seven, eight men he counted; all sitting on the ground except one who stood in the centre and appeared to be talking. He crossed to the other tent. The entrance flap was not fastened, so he lifted it, glanced inside, and saw the rifles, laid out on a ground sheet. He counted a dozen altogether and guessed that there was one per man and four spares. Even AK47s would sometimes jam. On the ground alongside the rifles were the magazines. There seemed to be a good many of them and he wondered how many a man would be able to carry, as well as his rifle, when climbing a rock face. Next to the magazines were bayonets and the sight of them came as a shock to Ian. Bayonets could only mean that the assault force were expecting to have to kill when they entered the Castle. He could picture them slipping over the wall and creeping up behind the sentries. Bayonets were for silencing men, permanently.

As he was looking into the tent his head

and shoulders were inside the flap and when he backed out of it, straightening to stand erect, a bent arm slid round his throat. A hand caught his hair roughly and pulled him round. For a brief instant he stared into a man's black face. Then he felt a sharp, chopping blow to the side of his neck and was falling, his mind spiralling into unconsciousness.

*   *   *

'What have we here?' the black man asked, grinning down at Ian.

'You're a bleeding cat, aren't you, Jimmy?' another man said. This one had a pink face. 'How many lives do you think you've got, eh, Jimmy?'

Ian realized that he was lying on the ground. He felt sick and dizzy and knew he had been asleep, was still in a nightmare, with black figures surrounding him, black enough to be demons, dressed in black and all except one with black faces.

The man whose face had not been blackened had grizzled red hair and bushy eyebrows. He said, 'Thick. That's what you are, Jimmy. Fucking stupid! You coming nosing around here looking for trouble. Well, you've had your lot this time, mate.'

'What are you going to do with him?' one of the other men asked. He drew his hand across his throat in an expressive gesture.

'We'll ask the old man. Give him a bell. Who's got the bleeding phone?'

'The general?'

'Who else? The boss has scarpered; gone to ground. Don't know why. The general shouldn't be far away. He must be getting near the rendezvous.'

He was handed a mobile phone and Ian watched as he punched out a number. He heard Craig explaining the situation, how this guy had sneaked up on them, was nosing into the tent, must have seen the rifles and other gear. Then Craig was silent, listening impassively to what the general was saying, a soldier listening to orders.

'He says there's to be no more killing,' he told the other men as the call ended. 'We're to leave him here tied up. As he says, in a couple of hours it'll be too late for our friend here to interfere. And who's going to find him here at this time of night?'

Ian tried to get up from the ground. They were in the larger tent now and he must have been dragged along the wet grass. The side of his neck ached and the whole of one shoulder was numb. When he tried to rise, the man standing nearest to him pushed him down by stamping on his chest.

'Tie the bastard up,' Craig said. 'Securely, mind, and gag him. And jump to it. We've wasted too much time already.'

Two men tied Ian's ankles and his hands together behind his back with rope. When he tried to resist a third man kicked him in the groin. Craig handed them a roll of brown sticky tape of the type used to secure parcels and they gagged Ian by sticking one strip across his lips and two more diagonally over his whole mouth. Then they dragged him by his feet into the smaller tent. As they did, he could see the other men pulling on black balaclavas and loading the rifles, magazines, and bayonets into the minibus. Finally, almost as an afterthought, one of the men slackened the ropes which held up the tent, allowing it to collapse on him. He heard the engine of the minibus being started and the straining of its engine as the tyres slipped on the wet ground.

The canvas of the tent smelt of damp and of smoke from a wood fire, with just a hint of human sweat. When it lay on him, Ian felt he was suffocating, which was perhaps what Sergeant-Major Craig had hoped might happen. After much painful wriggling he managed to twist his body so that he was lying on his side and his lips and nostrils were free of the walls of the tent. He wondered whether there was enough air in the small space to keep him alive and decided that he must keep wriggling his shoulders so that more air would be admitted.

After a time he seemed to grow accustomed to the discomfort and to his helplessness. What angered and depressed him was the knowledge of his own stupidity. He should have driven directly to Edinburgh. Had he stopped to think he would have realized that looking for the place where the assault force might be assembling was only pandering to curiosity, to an urge to prove to himself that he had been right. If he had driven straight to Edinburgh he might have arrived in time to alert the police or security service. Surely in Edinburgh he would have found somebody who would have believed his story.

He had no way of knowing for how long he lay trussed up beneath the collapsed tent; certainly an hour, perhaps more. He may have even slept for a time. When he heard voices and someone moving not far from him, he could not believe it. This must be another dream or nightmare. The sounds persisted so he tried to shout and attract attention, but his cries were so muffled that he abandoned the attempt and concentrated instead on trying to twist his body so that the tent would move.

'He must be somewhere here,' he heard a man's voice saying. 'That was his father's car by the road. I recognized it.'

'There! Beneath that tarpaulin. Something moved. I'm sure of it.'

When the tent was dragged off him and he saw Isobel standing above him with Bruce beside her, he tried to laugh. Only a laugh would defuse the happiness which threatened to explode inside him.

CHAPTER SEVENTEEN

'Did you say there are eight men?' Isobel asked Ian.

'Nine when the gallant general joins them.'

'Nine men can't possibly hope to take Edinburgh Castle.'

'They might well do,' Bruce said. 'The Castle has no garrison. The guard is only a handful of men, not more than a platoon, sent in from Redford Barracks. If armed men could scale the walls, they could surprise the guard.'

The three of them were heading for Edinburgh in Bruce's car. They had left Ian's father's car by the road where he had parked it, for Sergeant-Major Craig and his men had slashed its tyres, presumably as a precaution in case Ian managed to free himself, although it might equally well have been through malice. Isobel was sitting next to Bruce and from time to time she would glance over her shoulder at Ian, as though to reassure herself that he was all right. He had already told them of the attempt that had been made to kill him that evening as he drove towards Ardnadaig.

'What about security?' he asked Bruce. 'Surely with the Queen in Edinburgh security must be red hot.'

'It is, but mainly around Holyroodhouse. Even a Scot Nat mouse couldn't get within a hundred yards of the gate. Though it's the IRA that are the main worry.'

'And they have made their protest in Glasgow.'

'Twice. A second bomb exploded in Queen Street Station this evening.'

The authorities, Bruce told them, had thought that the IRA might try to plant a bomb in Edinburgh Castle, which would explode before the Queen entertained her EC guests to dinner there. The Castle, the Esplanade, and all streets leading up to them had been rigorously searched every morning and again at night for the past week. The Castle had been closed to visitors for the past three days and the staff of GOC Scottish Command, who worked there during the day, had been vetted and revetted and searched whenever they arrived or left.

'People are saying that they have all the staff under twenty-four-hour surveillance, including the Governor of the Castle,' Bruce said, 'but it's probably an exaggeration.'

'The bombs in Glasgow were exploded as part of an agreement between Sandy Ballantine and the IRA,' Ian told them. 'At least no one was killed.'

'What do you suppose Scotland Arise's plan of attack will be?' Isobel asked.

'Once the assault force have scaled the walls they will take out the sentries and the rest of the guard.'

'Kill them?'

'No, I'm sure they will be able to overcome the guard without violence,' Ian replied reassuringly, although he still remembered the bayonets he had seen lying in the tent.

'I agree,' Bruce said. 'Violence and certainly any killing would alienate popular support.'

'Meanwhile the balance of the force will have moved into Edinburgh with the equipment it needs. My guess is that they will come in trucks disguised as Army transport.' Ian remembered the skill with which the men who had almost killed him on the road to Ardnadaig had disguised themselves. 'Once the guard is taken, the trucks will drive across the Esplanade and into the Castle. It could be as simple as that.'

'Then the plan could work,' Isobel remarked. 'No one will be imagining that anyone would be crazy enough even to wish to capture Edinburgh Castle.'

They were approaching Edinburgh and could see the outlines of the Forth Bridge against the night sky. The wind was from the north-east and as cold as it almost always was in Edinburgh, but the clouds were broken, suggesting that sleet or snow were unlikely. The traffic in and out of the city had dwindled to a trickle.

'I wish I had been at home when you rang earlier,' Bruce said to Ian. 'I could have scooped everyone with this story; the nationals, TV, everyone. Can't you see the headline? "Scot Nats storm Edinburgh Castle"?'

Bruce had tried to contact his paper, stopping at a phone box in Dunkeld to make a call. He had been unable to reach anyone who would listen to him for the night desk was awash with calls from Glasgow. Extra reporters had been pulled in, but it would be hours before they could cope with the crisis and in any case the next day's papers might well have already been put to bed.

'Do you think we'll reach the Castle in time to see it taken?' Isobel asked.

'It's unlikely. My guess is that they would have begun the assault soon after the Castle floodlights were switched off.'

'That's usually at about one,' Bruce said.

'They might be leaving them on a while longer in honour of the Heads of State.'

'And pay for all that extra electricity? The

city fathers would have a collective heart attack!' As a Glaswegian Bruce believed that all Edinburgh folk were parsimonious.

As they drove through Barnton they saw nothing to suggest that anything had happened to disturb Edinburgh's suburbs. Bruce turned on the car's radio, for the programmes would surely be interrupted with news flashes were the Castle to be taken. All they heard were the anodyne sounds of sentimental music, supposedly for easy listening.

When they reached West End, Bruce turned into Lothian Road and made his approach to the Castle up Castle Terrace and Johnston Terrace. Soon they saw the Castle above them, silent on its rock.

'If the Castle has been taken surely the police would have set up road blocks to prevent anyone approaching it,' Isobel remarked.

'Only if they knew it had been taken.'

Bruce parked the car by the side of the road just before they reached the top of the hill and the three of them climbed the flight of steps which led up to Castlehill. From there they could see across the Esplanade to the entrance to the Castle. The chain had been put across the entrance to the Esplanade as it always was at night to prevent motorists parking there. Usually two armed sentries would be posted by the chain but there were none that night. They could just make out the figures of two sentries guarding the bridge which led to the archway in the Gatehouse, which was where they usually stood during the day.

While they were standing there a uniformed policeman came up from behind them. He had seen them as he patrolled the Lawnmarket and was curious to know what they were doing. Visitors often stopped to gaze across the Esplanade at the imposing entrance to the Castle, but usually not at half-past three in the morning.

'Good evening, sir, madam.'

'Good evening, officer.'

'May I ask what you are doing here?'

'Just checking to see that the Castle is safe,' Bruce said facetiously.

The policeman looked at him with patient resignation. They had been drinking, he probably believed. The Scandic Crown hotel further down the Royal Mile had a piano bar which stayed open until two in the morning. Young people who went there, yuppies they liked to be called, were usually well behaved but there were always exceptions.

'Are you Edinburgh people?' he asked them.

To cut short the discussion Bruce took out his press pass and showed it to the man. 'It's all right, officer. We were just about to leave.'

'Maybe that's as well, sir,' the policeman said and then he added, 'if you were looking for a story you would be better in Glasgow.'

'I was; earlier this evening.'

'Then you'll have heard about the second bomb?'

'At Queen Street Station? Aye. Were there any casualties?'

'Only minor injuries caused by flying glass fragments. We had a warning early enough to close the station.'

They chatted for a time about the Glasgow bombings. A friend of the policeman's had been killed when an IRA bomb had exploded in London and he had no sympathy for the Irish. While the three of them were talking, they suddenly heard a loud voice boom out from the direction of the Castle.

'One, two, three, four, testing.' There was a pause for a few seconds then the counting was resumed. 'Seven, eight, nine, ten, testing. Over and out.'

'They'll be testing the loudspeakers,' the policeman said after he and the others had recovered from their surprise.

'I didn't know they had amplifying equipment fitted in the Castle,' Bruce said.

'It's a funny time to be testing it,' Ian remarked.

'They'll be wanting to make sure it's all in good working order,' the policeman told them. 'Tomorrow's a big day for the Castle

271

and for Edinburgh too.'

★   ★   ★

When Ian took off his shirt Isobel gasped. His chest and upper arms were covered in bruises from the impact of the steering-wheel when his car had been hurled into the tree. A weal, red and ugly, showed where the mercenary from Scotland Arise had trodden on him. Ian had not been conscious of the bruises nor of his aching muscles when they had arrived in Edinburgh. Now they had stiffened up and he could feel the pain when he moved.

'My God, what have they done to you, you poor thing!'

Isobel had already undressed and was sitting on the edge of the bed. When she saw the bruises she reached up and stroked his chest gently. The touch of her fingers did nothing for the aching muscles but sharpened a desire that was almost as painful.

When he went to take her in his arms, she asked him, 'Are you sure you're feeling up to this?'

'If you were more observant,' he replied smiling, 'you would have noticed that I am.'

'So I see,' she said and laughed.

In any other girl, Ian thought, the laugh would have sounded lascivious, but coming from Isobel it was natural, an expression of the pleasure she knew they would give each other. When she took his hands and raised them to her breasts, all thoughts of pain vanished. He remembered her anxiety and awkwardness the first time they had made love and was moved to see her growing confidence in her own body and in him. Fatigue did nothing to diminish his own desire, but only seemed to add to the intensity of its pleasure.

After they made love they must have slept, but only briefly, for it was still dark when the radio woke them. Ian had left it switched on, playing the same soothing music as they heard when driving into Edinburgh, thinking perhaps that if there was any dramatic announcement it would wake him. He was right.

'We are interrupting this programme,' the announcer said, 'to give you a news flash. It is reported that a group of armed men have broken into Edinburgh Castle and are holding the guard hostage. No details of the incident have yet been given. As soon as we receive any more information a further announcement will be made.'

The broadcast continued with the same record that had been playing when it was interrupted. Ian could not help laughing aloud at the incongruity of listening to 'Strangers in the Night', with Isobel beside him and knowing that not more than a mile away a handful of Scots were making history. Whatever the outcome of Scotland Arise's reckless adventure might be, news of it would sweep through the world.

His laughter woke Isobel. 'What is it?' she asked sleepily.

'They've taken the Castle.'

Immediately she was fully awake; she sat up in bed and turned up the volume of the radio. 'Was anyone killed?'

'They didn't say. It was one of those castrated official announcements that tell you almost nothing.'

'Perhaps they don't know yet.'

'They only know what Scotland Arise have told them. The assault force must have been in the Castle for hours now. They will have telephoned the radio stations and the TV companies and told them that they are holding the Castle. What's the time? Seven-thirty? Perfect timing! Just as the whole of Edinburgh is getting out of bed.'

'Let's get up too. I can't sleep through this.' They pulled on some clothes, went into the living-room and turned on the television set. A former actress, no longer young, was demonstrating exercises which guaranteed to remove flab, tone up stomach muscles, and restore the bloom of youth to ageing bodies. Ian wished the actress could have seen Isobel's body, for that might have shamed her into silence.

'I'll go and make coffee,' he said.

When he had made coffee, poured them both orange juice, and returned to the living-room, the actress was still exercising. She had been joined by a small group of middle-aged women, some of them grotesquely fat, who were trying to imitate her movements.

'This is unbelievable!' Isobel complained. 'Fiddling with their fannies while Rome burns.'

It was not until the eight o'clock breakfast news programme began that they heard anything more. Even then they had to wait until the programme's graphic titles had been elaborately constructed on the screen. Finally the presenter appeared.

'Good morning,' he said. 'The Secretary of State for Scotland has just made the following announcement. "During the night a force of armed men climbed into Edinburgh Castle and surprised the guard, taking them prisoner. I have been informed that the men are part of an organization which calls itself Scotland Arise and that it has announced its intention to hold the Castle and prevent Her Majesty The Queen from dining there with her foreign guests this evening. The Army and the security services are now planning the action required to remove the men from the Castle. I shall make a further statement in due course. In the meantime, in the interests of public safety, the Castle has been isolated and all streets leading to it are being closed. I regret the inconvenience which this will cause and assure you all that we will act with all speed to bring this state of emergency to an end as soon as possible."'

The presenter put down the sheet of paper from which he had been reading and continued, 'I will now give you the headlines of other national and international news. Following that we will be going to our Edinburgh studio, where we hope to have an officer from the City Police who will be able to give details of arrangements that are being made to control traffic in the city.'

Neither Isobel nor Bruce wished to hear the news headlines. They left the television on but turned down the volume of the sound.

'What will happen now, do you think?' Isobel asked.

'Scotland Arise will make its demands known. General Wreford will have finished the proclamation that Sandy started to write. He'll send it to the government, with copies to the media no doubt, to make sure it gets the widest possible publicity.'

'And how will the government respond?'

'My guess is that it will play for time, pretending that it is prepared to negotiate.

276

The only other option is to storm the Castle. That would be unacceptable, as long as the TV cameras of the world are trained on Edinburgh. Can you imagine the uproar if men were killed?'

That morning the world news was given cursory treatment on Scottish television. Soon the newscaster was back on the screen, talking at length of the Castle's capture, even though he had nothing new to report. Meanwhile the police had been working swiftly and presently they were able to screen a map of Edinburgh which showed how the Castle was to be isolated. All streets leading to it or to the Royal Mile were to be closed to pedestrians as well as to traffic.

When he saw the map Ian exclaimed, 'This will cause chaos. Half of Edinburgh won't be able to get to work.'

'Scotland Arise has given us an extra public holiday. That will be popular.'

When Isobel left the room to take a shower and dress, Ian remembered the brown envelope which he had found in his father's car. He had retrieved it from the glove compartment after Bruce and Isobel had freed him and brought it with him to Edinburgh.

The smaller envelope seemed to hold only papers. The first ones he looked at were photocopies of official forms. C88s were forms that had to be completed giving the destination of all Scotch whisky that was being exported. In addition the volume and value of the shipments had to be recorded.

Ian found three C88s, all very similar and all giving details of consignments of malt whisky that had been exported, two by Loch Maree distillery and one by Glen Torridon distillery. The consignee in all cases was a company in Aruba. Looking at them Ian remembered reading in *The Spirit of Whisky* a graphic account of how Scotch arriving in Aruba and Curaçao was transferred almost at once to small boats and smuggled into Venezuela and Colombia. The other papers in the envelope appeared to be copies of invoices from a firm of travel agents.

Before Ian had time to study them, Bruce telephoned. 'Are you two out of bed yet?' he asked.

Ian wondered whether the way Bruce had worded his question implied that he had assumed Isobel and he had got out of bed together. 'Of course. We've been watching television, waiting to find out what's going to happen up at the Castle.'

'You'll have a better view from where I'm taking the two of you. I'll pick you up in half an hour.'

'What is this?'

'Some very important people want to talk to you.'

CHAPTER EIGHTEEN

Bruce took the two of them up Princes Street and through police barriers at the end of North Bridge to a building not far from Holyroodhouse which Ian never knew existed. Armed police were stationed outside the entrance, but the three of them were allowed to enter when Bruce showed some kind of pass that he was carrying, the same pass that he had shown at the police road blocks.

The room on the top floor of the building into which they were taken looked like an operations room for a military campaign. It was in fact an operations room, but one from which the security for the Queen's visit to Edinburgh and the summit meeting was being controlled. Illuminated maps of Edinburgh, mounted on glass screens, were ranged across two walls. One was a map of the whole city and it was flanked by larger-scale maps each showing no more than a few streets. Blue lights picked out the key features on each map, while a whole series of orange lights marked certain buildings and street intersections. Green lights had been used to indicate places where television cameras had been mounted to keep virtually the whole centre of Edinburgh under permanent surveillance.

Television screens occupied the whole of a third wall. One large one, mounted in the centre of the wall, was monitoring the day's BBC programmes. Pictures from a camera trained on the Castle and Esplanade were relayed to another large screen. On a table running along the length of the remaining wall a row of men and women, all in civilian clothes, were seated at a battery of telephones, taking incoming calls and transferring the information that was being phoned in on to the maps. Half a dozen men, two in Army uniform, two very senior police officers, and two in civilian clothes, were watching the screens. These were the men, Ian guessed, who together were in control of the massive security precautions that had been put in train for the Queen's visit. The atmosphere in the room was not as frenetic, or even as busy, as one might have expected.

The BBC was screening a programme for schools and the attention of most of the people watching was concentrated on the television picture of the Castle. As far as Ian could tell there was no one moving either in the Castle or on the Esplanade. A huge white banner had been fixed above the archway in the gatehouse, on which, between two Scottish flags, one at each end, the name SCOTLAND ARISE was printed in huge letters. The shot of the Castle was being taken from a long range, perhaps from a camera mounted on the old Outlook Tower at the top of the Royal Mile, where the camera obscura was now housed.

When one of the men in the group which seemed to be in charge saw Bruce, Isobel and Ian arrive, he came over to them. 'Are these your friends?' he asked Bruce.

'Yes. Ian Blackie and Isobel Gillespie.'

'I'm Mackenzie.'

The man shook their hands. He must have been almost fifty and was dressed in a grey business suit, but there was something in his manner, the assurance which discipline and an absolute confidence in one's vocation can instil, that suggested a military background.

Bruce pointed at the shot of the Castle on the large screen. 'I'm surprised you have no TV cameras in the Castle,' he remarked.

'We have. Batteries of them ready for tonight's dinner, but those chaps have immobilized them. They're no fools,' Mackenzie replied. Then he added, 'Let's go somewhere where we can talk.'

He led them into a small office which adjoined the main room and in which there was a table and chairs. A young policeman carrying a notebook came with them.

'Now tell me everything you know about this mob,' Mackenzie said and the others looked at Ian.

Ian began by describing how his father had become suspicious of General Ballantine's death and of how he too had visited Ardnadaig. Mackenzie interrupted him but not impatiently.

'Don't tell me how you found out what you know.' He smiled. 'That will make a good story for your friend Bruce to print later. Just tell me what you know about the outfit in the Castle; how many men there are, what weapons they have, who's in command, and anything else.'

Ian told him that the force Scotland Arise had trained amounted to forty-eight men, that they were equipped with AK47 assault rifles and commanded by General Douglass Wreford, with Sergeant-Major Fergus Craig acting as his NCO.

'Do they have any other weapons?'

'I wouldn't know, I'm afraid.'

'Would they have been able to carry any more weapons?' Isobel asked.

'We believe that they may have taken all the equipment they need, and rations as well, in stolen Army trucks. We have had a report that a convoy of five trucks were seen in the suburbs of the city early this morning.'

'Scotland Arise has formed a provisional government,' Ian told Mackenzie. 'Do you wish to know the names of its members?'

Before Mackenzie had time to answer a young man, also in civilian clothes, looked round the doorway into the office. 'You'll want to watch this, sir,' he told Mackenzie. 'General Wreford is going to make a statement on television.'

They all went back into the operations room. On one of the large screens they saw a BBC presenter who was explaining that General Douglass Wreford, commander of the force that had captured Edinburgh Castle during the night, was about to make a statement. The other large screen was showing the same inanimate shot of the Castle, featuring the banner over the gatehouse, as it had been doing for the past hour.

When Wreford appeared he did not look like a man who had scaled the walls of a castle and been active all night. He was wearing his Army uniform and, Ian had to admit, wearing it with dignity. He began to speak, not reading from a script but looking straight at the cameras.

'Good morning. I'm Douglass Wreford and I'm speaking to you from Edinburgh Castle, a Scot speaking to Scots. As many of you will know by now, last night a small force of Scottish patriots, which I have the honour to command, took over control of Edinburgh Castle. We did so without violence, no one was hurt, no shot was fired. Although the Castle guard are now our prisoners, I sense that many of them are willing prisoners, happy to have put down their arms in the cause of what is a historic event, a proud moment in the history of our country. There will be few among you who have not the words of the Declaration of Arbroath printed on your hearts. Let me remind you of them.'

The General stopped speaking as an extract from the Declaration appeared on the television screen.

It is in truth not for glory, nor riches, nor honours that we are fighting, but for freedom—for that alone, which no honest man gives up but with life itself.

Wreford's face reappeared on the screen and he continued, 'Almost three hundred years ago our freedom, the freedom of Scotland, was taken from us. Since that time our country has been demeaned and humiliated, left powerless to watch its riches being squandered, its heritage dissipated.'

'Christ!' an officer in the uniform of a general shouted. 'He's not speaking from the Castle!'

'No,' Bruce said, 'what we're watching is a video.'

They watched as the video, carefully and professionally produced, continued with Wreford developing his theme. Over background shots of empty shipyards and docks, deserted coalmines and a run-down steelworks, he described how Scotland's wealth had been pillaged, her industries allowed to decay. Even its whisky distilleries were being run from London, New York, and Tokyo. Although the voice was that of General Wreford, Ian could see the hand of Montgomerie Banks in the making of the video. His firm would have the expertise and the contacts to be able to produce a video secretly and have it ready. No doubt it would have been handed in at the BBC studios that morning.

After the history lesson Wreford made his demands. 'Scotland Arise is not looking for confrontation. Nor do we mean any disrespect to Her Majesty. As soon as the Government makes an irrevocable commitment to grant our country independence we will lay down our weapons peacefully and allow the Queen and her guests into the Castle. More than that, we will provide her with a bodyguard this evening while she dines; a kilted bodyguard of true patriots, not of elderly aristocrats dressed up in Lincoln green.'

'That will get him drummed out of the brownies,' Bruce whispered, 'or at least out of the Archers.'

'How the hell did the BBC get hold of this?' Mackenzie demanded.

'More important, why are they showing

285

it?' the general, whose name Ian had gathered was Boothroyd, asked. 'They have no right to.'

'Give comfort to the enemy?' Bruce asked slyly. One had the impression that he was enjoying his morning.

'Exactly. Someone is going to lose his balls over this.'

At last the showing of the video was over. The BBC presenter told the world that normal programmes would now be resumed, but promised that as soon as they had any further news from Edinburgh Castle, they would broadcast it. The senior officials in the operations room looked glum, well aware that Scotland Arise had won its second victory. Not only had the Castle been hijacked but the media itself, God only knew how, had ensured that millions of viewers all round the world had watched Wreford's clever emotional appeal.

'Well, gentlemen,' Mackenzie asked the others, 'what do we do now? The TV people are clamouring for someone to go on the box and make a statement. And the Queen's secretary has been on the phone asking what the hell is going on.'

'We'll have to smoke them out.' Boothroyd had made up his mind. 'The longer they stay in the Castle, the more publicity they will be getting.'

'Not necessarily. We can issue an order for

a TV and radio blackout. We can cut off the telephone lines to the Castle.'

'Tonight's dinner need not be held in the Castle. They could switch it to Holyroodhouse.'

'Better to get them out. Quickly and quietly.'

'How? You can hardly shell the place or use armour.'

'From the air. I've already put the Army helicopters on alert.' Boothroyd looked pleased with himself. 'We can drop men in all over the Castle, on the flat roofs, everywhere. Forty-eight men can't protect the whole place.'

'We don't want shooting; mustn't make martyrs.'

'There'll be no shooting. That rabble will cave in once they see we mean business. I bet Wreford never thought of helicopters. He's a dinosaur.'

Even as they were talking they heard the distant drone of a helicopter. 'That's the first chopper,' Boothroyd said. 'I told them to put one up with cameras first, to carry out a reconnaissance.'

Presently one of the smaller TV screens that had so far been blank, was filled with an aerial view of the Castle. One could see the assault troops of Scotland Arise, some on the roof of the gatehouse, covering the Esplanade with rifles, others by the portcullis gate, more still around the half-moon battery and by the western defences. It seemed to Ian that they were expecting to be attacked but had no idea from where the attack would come.

A telephone rang and one of the general's aides answered it. 'The other choppers are airborne and will be here in five minutes, sir,' he told Boothroyd.

'Can we reach the Castle on that phone?' the general asked.

'No problem.'

It took longer than expected to get anyone to answer the call that was put through to the Castle. When a connection was made Boothroyd asked to speak to General Wreford. The idea that commanders facing each other in a conflict should speak to each other on the telephone struck Ian as bizarre. But then this was not war, only a mock war that had gone wrong.

'Wreford? This is Boothroyd,' the general said loudly. 'We are sending in an airborne force. You have ten minutes to surrender.' Wreford's response could not have been one the general wanted to hear for he went on, 'Oh, come on man! Don't be a bloody fool! Put down your weapons and come out. No one will be hurt.' Wreford was still apparently not prepared to surrender. Boothroyd said roughly, 'Right, you've had your chance.' Wreford's next reply seemed to disconcert Boothroyd. He put down the phone and looked at the others in the operations room.

'He says they have SAMS. Can that be true?'

'Surface to air missiles,' Bruce explained to Ian. 'Do you know if they have any?'

Ian was about to say that he did not know, then a sudden thought sparked. 'Would "javelins" be missiles?' he asked. 'There was a reference to javelins in the notes General Ballantine had made shortly before he was due to meet the IRA. And another reference to Lightweight MLs.'

'Multiple launchers for missiles! My God, they're mad!' Mackenzie exclaimed.

'Wreford would never use them,' Boothroyd said. 'He's bluffing. He'd not shoot down Scottish soldiers.'

As he was speaking they saw on the screen a shot of helicopters approaching Edinburgh. They were flying in line abreast, ten of them. Then they broke formation as they drew nearer to the Castle and began to circle it, though at a distance. The BBC had its own camera trained on the Castle now, also from a distance, showing only the deserted Esplanade, the banner across the gatehouse and the two sentries posted outside it. There was nothing in the picture to suggest that this was the scene of even a mock war, but the commentator was speaking in hushed tones, trying to heighten the drama.

'Send one chopper in,' Boothroyd ordered a soldier at the far end of the room who was sitting at a radio telephone and evidently was in touch with the helicopters.

'Are you sure that's wise?' Mackenzie asked.

One helicopter broke away from the others and headed for the centre of the city. Ian thought he could see soldiers in combat gear sitting ready by its doors. The note of its engine changed as it began to lose height, dropping slowly down towards the Castle.

The TV cameras hardly had time to pick out the Javelin missile as it was launched. It snaked into the sky, twisting to home in on its target. There was scarcely a need to bring its complicated guidance equipment into operation. The helicopter, a waddling duck, was an easy target.

Isobel shut her eyes and turned her face into Ian's shoulder as they saw the explosion, the huge ball of orange flame and fragments of metal and bodies falling out of the sky. The noise of the blast seemed to come almost minutes later. In the operations room no one spoke, watching the horror in stunned silence.

* * *

What followed only seemed like anti-climax
290

in contrast to the sickening drama they had been watching. A young man in the operations room, a civilian, began to weep. That released the tension and General Boothroyd began to swear, cursing Wreford with obscenities.

'Tell the helicopter pilots to back off, to keep out of range,' Mackenzie shouted to the radio telephone operator.

The television picture vanished from the BBC screen and it was almost a minute before the face of the presenter appeared and began mumbling incoherently that the programme would be discontinued.

'What do we do for an encore?' Mackenzie asked Boothroyd sarcastically. 'Any suggestions?'

'Someone will have to tell the Secretary of State,' someone said.

'He will have been watching it—if he's out of his bath yet, that is.'

'And the Queen must be informed.'

Gradually the shocked silence in the operations room was replaced by a frenzied activity. Soon every telephone in the room was in use, calls made, some refused.

'That was the press,' someone shouted. 'They say that Wreford's video is at this moment being shown on French TV.'

'What the hell are we supposed to do about it?' one of the police officers asked angrily.

'It will be screened all over Europe and networked in the United States. You can be sure of that.'

Mackenzie meanwhile had stepped into the adjoining office and was phoning the Secretary of State for Scotland. All the activity, the phone calls, the shouted instructions, it seemed to Ian, were just a smokescreen to hide indecision. The army officers were talking of strategy options, a sure sign that they had no idea of what they should do next.

Then suddenly a man at the telephone table shouted. 'It's Wreford. He says they're coming out. Surrendering.'

'Tell him to wait until we give the all-clear,' Boothroyd shouted back. 'I don't trust the bugger.'

Twenty minutes passed before two platoons of armed soldiers could be stationed at the top of the Royal Mile to cover Scotland Arise's assault troops as they left the Castle. They came out unarmed with their hands clasped at the back of their heads. Some of them had changed from whatever combat gear they had been wearing into kilts. Had they been preparing, Ian wondered, for what they thought would be a parade of honour that evening, guarding the Queen as she arrived at the Castle? Wreford led them out and one could see no defiance in him.

'Did Wreford say whether there had been any casualties?' Boothroyd asked Mackenzie.

'Only one. A Sergeant-Major Craig. He was shot dead.'

CHAPTER NINETEEN

For two days Edinburgh was in trauma, a divided city. On balance most of the sympathy lay with Scotland Arise. The Army had no right, people said, to send in helicopters in order to beat them into submission. People remembered that General Wreford had said that his men did not want a confrontation, that they would lay down their weapons peacefully. And had they not paid the Queen a courtesy, even though the many Scots who turned their noses up at royalty felt she did not deserve it? More than a few thought of Scotland Arise as a band of heroes for making a stand, for doing what all true Scots should do. Most people were convinced that the missile had been fired accidentally or only in panic.

The media were trying to make a martyr out of Fergus Craig. They pointed to his fine military record, to the work he had been doing to help soldiers who had been obliged to leave the Army. No one knew how he had been killed. In fact it had been Craig who, on

293

his own initiative and in a fit of psychopathic rage, had fired the missile and he had been shot on the orders of General Wreford to prevent him firing more. But the Army had preferred that this should not be known.

Then on the third day, just as feelings were beginning to weaken, the *Scotsman* published a sensational story. 'SCOTLAND ARISE FUNDED BY DRUG MONEY' was the headline, and the report went on to say that money raised by selling Scotch whisky to the drug barons of Colombia had been used to finance all the activities of Scotland Arise. Malt whisky from the two distilleries owned by the West Highland Scotch Whisky Company had been shipped to Colombia, via the Caribbean, where drug dealers had re-exported it to the United States. Single-malt whiskies under the labels of both distilleries were freely on sale in Florida.

None of the whisky was sold in Colombia and the operation was simply a way of laundering money made from the sale of drugs. To give it local interest, the story suggested that most of the illegal drugs now sold on the street in Edinburgh was known to be from Colombia.

Once the story appeared public sympathy for Scotland Arise rapidly wilted. Drugs were a sensitive subject, as people believed it was drug-taking that was responsible for the epidemic of Aids, which had reached greater proportions in Edinburgh than in any other city in Britain. There were demands for police action against the whisky company or, if that was not feasible, for a public inquiry. From the first report the story and public indignation snowballed. When it was revealed that the son of the Prime Minister had been responsible for selling the whisky to the drug dealers, the sensation became a political scandal. In Parliament there were demands for the resignation of Alisdair Buchanan.

As soon as Ian saw the story he phoned Bruce and asked him how the *Scotsman* had received its information.

'An anonymous tip-off,' Bruce replied, 'with some back-up material sent through the post.'

'Isn't that unusual? I thought people expected to be paid for stories.'

'Not everyone. There's no shortage of gratuitous malice, even in Edinburgh.'

Ian told him that he might be able to add something to the story and they arranged that Isobel and he should go and have supper with Bruce and Kirsten in their home that evening. When, once again before supper, Isobel was taken upstairs to admire the children, Ian showed Bruce what had been in the brown envelope which he had found in his father's car.

'Why don't we follow this up?' Bruce

asked him.

'How can we?'

'How about my asking Tristram Stewart for an interview? He seems to be the man who has been pulling the strings.'

'Will he agree?'

'He'll jump at it. They tell me he plans to return to parliament so he'll need all the publicity he can get. I'll fix it so you can come along too.'

The interview was as easy to arrange as Bruce had thought. Stewart invited them to meet him in the New Club the following evening. They met him in the Members' bar and Ian had the feeling that in spite of the sensation of Scotland Arise's attack on the Castle, nothing had changed. Stewart was full of the same bonhomie and self-assurance. In the Members' bar several of his friends came up to congratulate him on his selection as a parliamentary candidate for the next election. After they had finished their drinks he took Bruce and Ian to a room where business conversations could be held. These were not permitted in the bar or dining-room.

'It looks as though the election will be sooner than anyone would have expected,' he told Ian and Bruce. 'I'm told that Buchanan will be resigning before the end of next week.'

'Why are you not standing for the SNP?'

Bruce asked him. 'I rather thought your sympathies lay in that direction.'

'They do. That is, I'm in favour of an assembly for Scotland. But that shambles of Scotland Arise has discredited the nationalist movement, for the time being at least. In politics one has to be a realist.'

'Were you not involved with Scotland Arise yourself?'

'Only very tenuously. When I heard they were heading for a confrontation, I pulled out.'

'And what about the drug money. You were a director of the West Highland Scotch Whisky Company, were you not? You must have known what was happening.'

'Do you think I'm mad? If I had known what was being done, I would have stopped it.'

Ian knew that this was his cue. 'That isn't true, Mr Stewart, and you know it. It was you and your friend Montgomerie Banks who set up the whisky deal with the Colombians.'

Stewart stared at him. One could see that behind the stare his mind was busy, trying to assess how much Ian knew and how he could most safely respond. 'Where on earth did you get that idea from, Ian? Not from your father, surely?'

'Partly, yes.'

'I have no wish to be unkind, but the poor

chap's mind was disturbed just before he died, was it not?'

Ian fought back his anger. He wanted to hit the man, but that would achieve nothing. So he pulled the papers he had been carrying from his pocket.

'These are photocopies of shipping documents for the whisky that was sent to Colombia,' he told Stewart. 'They are dated at a time when you were still a director of the West Highland Scotch Whisky Company. And here are invoices from Westminster Confidential, the firm of your friend Banks. They cover the cost of two return first-class air tickets from London to Bogotá.'

'Oh yes,' Stewart said. 'And in whose names were the tickets issued?'

'Montgomerie Banks and Andrew Blackie. Using my father's name was a careless mistake, Mr Stewart. My father never travelled to Bogotá and he would be able to prove it. Unless of course you knew that he would soon be dead and not able to disprove that he was involved in the business. There is also a charge in the invoices for hotels and other expenses for the two of you in Maicao. Maicao is the smuggling centre of Colombia. It only exists for smuggling. You, with your former parliamentary contacts in the country, would easily have been able to set up the whisky deal with the drug barons.'

Now it was Stewart who was beginning to

lose his temper. He said to Bruce, 'I thought it was you who were supposed to be interviewing me. Did you bring your friend here just to accuse me?'

Ian was not prepared to allow him to wriggle free. 'Scotland Arise was my father's idea. You used it for your own ends. You arranged the deal with the Colombians to get at the Prime Minister through his son. You've ruined the career of an able politician and a good man just for private revenge.'

'It's rubbish! Paranoid rubbish!' Stewart said to Bruce. 'These scraps of paper prove nothing. And now, if you don't mind, we'll bring this interview to an end.'

When Ian and Bruce were walking along Princes Street together, Ian said, 'He'll get away with it, you know. That's what makes me sick.'

Stewart, he realized, had cleverly dissociated himself from Scotland Arise, stepping back at just the right moment. Being a member of a nationalist organization was not a crime and no one would be able to prove that he had been involved in the attack on Edinburgh Castle or the shooting down of the helicopter.

'It must have been Stewart who gave your paper the tip-off about the drug money,' he concluded. 'And he'll get away with it. He'll not face trial.'

'Not in a court of law,' Bruce replied, 'but

he may have forgotten that there is also trial by media.'

'You can't print all this. There's no evidence. He'd sue you.'

'Newspapers have ways of unearthing the truth. We can send people to Colombia, to Florida. We can find ways of examining the whisky company's records and accounts and correspondence. People can always be persuaded to talk. By the time we are finished Stewart will be dead, politically dead I mean. If we're lucky he might well finish up in jail.'

'Will the *Scotsman* go for it?'

'Why not?' Bruce said. 'Stewart has discredited Scottish nationalism, may have set it back years. My management won't like that.'

He set out for North Bridge to put in train the investigative journalism that would complete the political destruction of Tristram Stewart. Ian walked to Dean village and found Isobel working at the word processor. He admired her single-mindedness. Castles might fall and be recaptured but creative life had to go on.

'You've just missed the TV news,' she told him. 'The police have evidence that Fergus Craig made the bomb that killed Sandy.'

'What evidence?'

Craig, Isobel told Ian, had been living alone since his wife died, and when his house was searched, the police found supplies of explosives, detonators, and radio equipment. Another member of Scotland Arise's assault force, an expert in explosives had told how Craig had asked for his advice on how to make bombs and on how they could be detonated by remote control.

'So we were right about Craig,' Ian remarked, 'though it's a bit late for self-congratulation now.'

'How did the meeting with Tristram Stewart go?' she asked him.

Ian gave her a brief account of the interview and told her what Bruce intended to do. 'I don't always approve of the tactics of the press,' he said, 'but this time I do. It's only the media that can bring Stewart to justice—a rough kind of justice, but still justice.'

'You'll not forgive him, will you?'

'Nobody should. I'm certain it was he who gave the order for Sandy to be killed. Wreford never would have.'

Ian did not add that there would always be a question in his mind, a question to which he would never know the answer. Did Stewart persuade Dr MacBain to kill his father? There were ways of killing a person suffering from heart trouble and no inquest would be held if the doctor who signed the death certificate had been treating the dead person. For the past few days he had been wondering whether he should go to the authorities and ask for an inquest into his father's death, but had decided not to. An inquest and the sensation it must cause would only distress his mother. MacBain would pay in other ways, once the part he had played in Scotland Arise's conspiracy was known to the press.

'When did you guess what Stewart was doing?' Isobel asked him.

'Not until it was too late. He must have known that you and I were making enquiries about the murder of Sandy and that we knew of the existence of Scotland Arise, but he did very little except just keep an eye on us. He knew we would be too late to prevent the attack on the Castle. Then Montgomerie Banks came to visit me in Invermuir. He saw that I had a report which gave information about whisky exports and that I was reading a book which described how whisky was being smuggled into South America. It was only then that Stewart decided that I should be killed.'

'Thank Heavens it's over, anyway.'

Ian had no wish to talk any longer about Tristram Stewart or about the drama at the Castle. People would be talking of nothing else for days, for weeks even. He looked at Isobel and saw that she was wearing a baggy, shapeless dress rather like the one she had been wearing when they first met.

302

'You've bought a new dress,' he said.

'Yes. Don't you like it?'

'I can see it's sensible and practical, but I don't really think it suits you.'

'I could always take it off.'

They made love where they were, on the carpet. Not because of the urgency of their desire, nor through any wish for new experiences, but because it was a natural response to their need for each other. Ian found himself thinking it would always be that way.

Later, when they lay back, enjoying the luxury of idleness, Isobel suddenly asked him, 'Will you illustrate my new book for me?'

'You can't be serious.'

'I am. I found that sketch you did of the golden eagle chicks.'

Ian had forgotten about the sketch. 'I haven't the talent.'

'You have. Other illustrators have worked on my books, but I've never been satisfied with the results.' She looked at him earnestly. 'You will, won't you?'

'We'll talk about it later, but I'm making no commitment.'

He remembered then what she had said to him after they had made love for the first time. She was making no commitments, nor asking for any. That had only been a few days ago, but the world had changed.

'Do you remember what you said before about not making commitments?'

Isobel only nodded. He knew she was waiting.

'Do we need commitments,' he asked, 'spoken promises? In some miraculous way our lives have come together, fused, become one. Why don't we just make it permanent?'